A SEA STORY

Through My Mind's Eye

Book II

Robert Brunjes

TABLE OF CONTENTS

PROLOGUE

This story has been on my mind for a long time. I dreamed it. Now I have put it to paper. Many have asked what happened to Lady Catherine and Sir Robert, so here is the rest of my story. A SEA STORY. Sailing ships in particular "Man of War" has been a fascination of mine since I was a little guy. The rigging of ships models looked logical to me where others saw confusion. Wherever there was a sailing ship I found a way to get on board. Mystic Seaport, the USS Constitution, USS Constellation, the Eagle, any sailing ship piqued my interest. This journey has become a labor of love. I am not a writer nor claim to be one, but it was important to me to get this story told. The names, places, and ideas in this book do not represent anyone living or dead. The places and ideas are a figment of my active imagination. This book was written on my iPhone mostly in the hours of darkness. For those who still read and dwell in the British Navy of 1800, and there are many, I apologize for any nautical misrepresentations and gladly accept twelve lashes at the grating. Enjoy this SEA STORY, through MY MINDS EYE.

AT ANCHOR

Two bells in the afternoon watch

HMS *Lightning,* a 24 gun frigate, had been anchored at Spithead for the last four days waiting for the latest gale to subside in the channel. This year 1801 had been the worst winter for storms in anyone's memory. Four of His Majesty's ships had been lost this winter on blockade duty. Spithead was full of ships waiting to get to sea.

HMS *Lightning* had a new captain. Commander Lord Leslie Nibley. His father controlled the purse strings in Parliament and he was one of a few that had gotten the coveted command of a frigate as a Master and Commander. The Admiralty had given Nibley a most capable First Lieutenant George Howe grandson of the famous Sir Richard Howe Admiral of the fleet until his death in 1799. He was now the last of the family to be in the King's uniform.

Aboard the *Lightning*, the new captain was eager to get underway. They had a passenger, one of the commissioners of the admiralties victualling board. He needed to discuss, with the Admiral of the Fleet off Brest, getting rations to the fleet under these weather conditions.

Captain Nibley called for his First Lieutenant. "We must get underway immediately." Lieutenant Howe could not believe it. "Sir no ship has left this anchorage in three days and there are a number of 74's who have not ventured out in this storm." Nibley in his arrogant tone, "I am ordering you to get us underway. The Admiral is waiting for the commissioner's arrival off Brest." The First Lieutenant still could not believe it. "Sir in this storm the fleet will be off Ushaut or worse. I must protest. This is madness." Nibley could see his authority was being undercut with the commissioner present. "That is an order and if you can't carry it out I will relieve you of your duties." Lieutenant Howe stormed out of the cabin for the deck. "Sailing Master prepare to get underway." The sailing master looked at him in shock. "SIR?"

"It appears that our illustrious captain will relieve me if we do not get underway"

"This is madness, Sir. I will call for the storm jibs and three reefs in the mainsails. ALL HANDS ON DECK."

The sailing master knew this would be a dicey move even with a trained crew. This one was on its first voyage and half the crew were landsmen with no experience. The sailing master looked at his First Lieutenant, "This is not going to end well."

Lord Nibley asked his servant to get dinner ready. "I wished to dine with my guest while the waters were calmer."

In a half-hour, they had the ship ready for sea. Lieutenant Howe reported to the great cabin. "Sir the ship is ready for Sea. The anchor is up and down." Nibley looked confused. "Well get underway!"

"Sir in all my years in the navy I have never left port without the captain on the quarterdeck."

"Well, there is a first time for everything. As you can see we are in the middle of our dinner."

The commissioner looked on with an oh my God look on his face.

"Very well. I will note it in the log." The Lieutenant returned to the quarterdeck and advised the sailing master, "Break the anchor loose, cat it, and get underway."

On the nearby 74 at anchor, the Lieutenant of the watch called for his Captain. "Sir that frigate is heading to sea." The captain looked at it through the glass and stated, "The captain of that frigate is either the best sailor in the British Navy or a fool." He suspected it was the latter.

HMS *Lightning* turned into the teeth of the storm. The ship ate the waves all night. By morning they had made less than ten leagues. The sailing master and the First Lieutenant never left the deck. Lieutenant Howe went with the morning report to the Captain's cabin. The commissioner was on his knees holding a bucket. Captain Nibley looked no better. Mr. Howe had a bit of a smile thinking, "I bet they both regret last night's meal." He reported to his Captain their position and any orders for the morning watch. Nibley had none. Howe returned to the deck to relieve the Sailing Master. They agreed to steer South-Southwest. It would not get them any closer to Brest but would prevent the ship from taking more of this continuous beating. The Captain never came on deck. They remained with double reefed storm sails and had made less then fifteen leagues headway all day. It was a miracle they had lost no one overboard so far. Half the crew was seasick the other half was scared out of their wits.

The First Lieutenant briefed the rest of the officers in the gun room. The Sailing Master commented that they were lucky to have made it through the night without floundering. He hoped their luck would hold out. He and Lieutenant Howe went to the great cabin to talk to the Captain. The commissioner was on his back on the floor. Nibley was seated at his desk. "How soon would they be off Brest and the fleet?" asked Nibley. Howe's only reply was, "maybe a few days if the storm weakens. They were heading South-Southwest and could not make the turn East until the winds were more favorable." Nibley was beside himself with anger. As they left the Sailing Master's only comment was, "Bloody hell Sir, with that man as captain we will never see England again."

They fought their way across the channel for three days and finally made the turn toward Brest. Howe knew the fleet would not be there as the storm had scattered them for twenty-five leagues and more. The front door was open for the French to break out and head to sea. On the seventh night, the lookouts reported two sails to windward. Nibley ordered them to close on the sails. He was certain it was part of the fleet. Howe argued that they should try and achieve the weather gage on them in case they were French. Nibley would have none of it and returned to the cabin. As the weather cleared the lookout reported, "Deck there. They are two 74's flying French colors." *Lightning* had only one option and that was to run. The Sailing Master yelled, "ALL HANDS ON DECK. Make all sail possible." He knew their luck had run out. He told Howe they would be in the range of their bow chasers in less than half an hour. Howe was furious. He went to his cabin to get his sword and pistol and then went to confront Nibley. He told Nibley of their predicament. The commissioner could not believe it. Nibley did not know what to do. Howe told the captain, "If you will not act then I will." He was not going to lose his ship and went on deck.

The French ships started firing their bow chasers. One shot came directly through the stern windows not four feet from where Nibley sat. On deck, the First Lieutenant shouted, "We shall beat to quarter. Sailing Master bring us about."

Then a shot rang out and the First Lieutenant fell face-first to the deck with a deepening red stain on his back. Nibley stood there smoking gun in hand. "I'll not risk my life for a bloody ship. Heave to and strike our colors. That is an order." Everyone on deck was shocked beyond belief. Nibley went back to his cabin and got his personal papers and money. Then he just sat there.

He told the commissioner not to worry his father would have them back in England in no time. The commissioner just sat there asking himself, "What the hell just happened?"

The French with some difficulty got on board and took control of the ship. They searched Howe's body, took his silver-buckled shoes and his sword which had been worn by Admiral Lord Howe in times past. They unceremoniously dumped his body over the side. As they entered the great cabin Captain Nibley sat next to the lead-weighted mail and dispatch bag which should have been dumped over the side. He just stared out the remaining cabin windows as the rain hit the glass.

STORM AT HOME

Four bells in the evening watch

The same storm was hitting Southwest England and the valley of the Exe. The rain was striking the windows of the bedchamber at Black Stone Cottage with the same veracity.

The electricity between the young couple remained strong. It was a special bond. Every time they explored the contours of each other's body it was like the first time. It was a match made in heaven that would remain with them all the days of their lives.

After they would face each other and open the bond of best friends and discuss life as they could not in normal society with the pretense of everyday living. They spoke as if they were of one mind. There were no secrets or hidden feelings between them. Catherine explained all the goings on in the village. Robert had noticed that the atmosphere had changed. There were many more people in town that he did not know and were very sullen. His lovely wife explained that with enclosure many families had been driven off the land after losing their leaseholds that most had for generations. They had no place to go. Most of the older generation had accepted their fate, but the younger members felt ill-used and blamed the Lords and landholders for their despair. Robert had seen this before on ship and it had to be dealt with before it turned into mutiny.

Across the village as the storm raged Lambert Hancock was working late in his study reviewing the accounts of his businesses. He was doing very well except for his enterprise in Winsford.

His son in law George who would be Viscount Torrington someday, married to Elizabeth, was overseeing the business for him. He could not figure it out but was losing a considerable amount of money. He would have to look into it after his trip North to meet with the rest of the Hancock clan as they did each year to discuss their considerable coal mining interests.

At the smithy, Tom Davies and John Hicks were sharing Mr. Davies's two rooms above the stable. Although Mr. Hicks was an educated man and Mr. Davies a tradesman, their common bond to the captain and both being sailors made them very compatible messmates.

The storm eventually moved on and the village came alive with activity. Catherine was still learning the habits of her Navy husband and his followers.

Man of war sailors were very self-conscious of cleanliness and appearance. Mr. Hicks made everything shine in the cottage. There was not a speck of dust anywhere. He also saw to Robert's wardrobe like he was a valet. Both John and Tom were lord protectors of the cottage and Cathrine. She really did have a staff with Rose in the kitchen and the men taking care of the cottage. She and her aunt Mimmie felt like royalty. Catherine was also concerned that her husband, always the in charge Captain would be so at home. It was the exact opposite. Robert loved life at home and left the running of the household to his bride. They would be married for almost four years, but the honeymoon continued.

The post rider came with the latest mail for the cottage and in it were Robert's orders to take command of the sea fencibles for the Devon Coast. He had a Lieutenant and yeoman stationed at Exmouth on the coast. Also, there was a packet from his prize agent. Robert sent word for John Hicks to come up to the cottage.

"You wanted to see me, sir?"

"Yes please sit down John. I have news from my prize agent at Lloyd's. I had Mr Waterhouse look into the cloud that has been hanging over your life. Please forgive me if I have overstepped, but I am completely aware of the circumstances of your debt. It is most regrettable when the people you trust most, your partner in business, and your wife run off with the proceeds of a loan you obtained to expand your copy-write business in London. In life we can't go back only forward. I have seen to the debt and it is paid. The cloud that has hung over your life is gone. You are a free man, John Hicks."

Robert handed him the letter of release from the debt. John was speechless at first then the rush of emotions took over. "Sir debtors prison and then being released to the press-gang was the low point of my life. Then I met you Sir and my new life began. I shall be forever in your debt. Never in my wildest dreams could I have imagined the new life I have as your clerk and servant. I can do nothing else."

"John I am honored to have you with me, but there is much more that you can do here. I have talked to the Magistrate and Mr. Hancock and both can use your services. That will help put you in funds. However, when you are not with me and the sea fencibles or assisting at the cottage I would like you to help my aunt and uncle with running the Tally Ho. The war will not last forever and our affairs here in Riverton will need our attention."

"I am honored to be serving with you, Sir."

"You are part of our family Mr Hicks, as much as Tom Davies is. We will see what life brings us. It is always full of surprises."

"It does indeed Sir." John Hicks was a happy man. He now had found his place in the world.

He was sailing with a following sea into the bright sunshine of life. As he left Catherine came into the dining room and gave her husband a kiss. "You are a fine man Sir Robert" as she smiled. He responded, "He was only as good as his partner in life made him, Lady Catherine." The whole squadron was sailing full and bye.

THE SEA FENCIBLES

Two bells in the afternoon watch

Robert made his first trip to Exmouth to visit with his new command. They were located at the old fortress that guarded the mouth of the river. He and Hicks had to use a hired boat to get across the river. The old cannons guarded the entrance to the harbor, but Robert was not sure if they had been fired this last century. After walking across the grounds they entered the building against the inner wall. There was a man sitting at a table by the door who jumped to attention when he saw the Post Captain's uniform. "Good afternoon Sir. I am Yeoman Gosport. How may I help you?"

"I am Captain Burnes, your new commander. Where is your Lieutenant?"

"He is in town with the Lieutenant of the press-gang Sir."

"Would you get him for me please." The older overweight sailor jumped up. "Aye Sir. I will have him here in a jiffy." Out the door he went.

Robert looked to Mr. Hicks. "We must remember that we are not on a King's ship and most of these men who serve are volunteers who get a sixpence a day plus relief from the press-gang." They waited. Soon a very young Lieutenant approached. "Sir, Lieutenant John Maxfield at your service." Robert estimated that he was about twenty years old and probably this was his first duty since getting his step. "I am Captain Robert Burnes your new commander. This is Mr. Hicks, my clerk. Would you show us around the command." The young officer showed him the buildings including the armory and the four gun emplacements. After returning to the building he asked for his muster book and journal. "When is your next muster? What is your training plan? How many men show up for duty?"

Maxfield answered with enthusiasm. "All most all report for muster. They fear the press-gang. Some of the local fishermen miss duty if the fishing is good. They can all use the sixpence a day. Next muster will be Friday." The Lieutenant had to tell it like it is. "Sir, your predecessor only came to muster a few times. All he asked was for the monthly report to be on time. He never gave me a plan of action so I drill the men in small arms, the cutlass and the like, but that is all."

Robert smiled. "Thank you for your honesty. We will try and do better."

That night at the local inn they had dinner with Lieutenant Maxfield. He discovered that this young man had come up the hard way. He had six years of school before he ran away to the sea. He started as a ship's boy at eleven. His captain recognized his potential and promoted him to a midshipman. He had no sponsor or money so it was a very lean existence and lived off the charity of others. He made his step on his second try and was put ashore with no ship in his future. The Port Admiral took pity on him and got him this assignment. He now lived on £8 per lunar month which was no easy task off ship.

They were enjoying dinner when Robert noticed that an older man with a pretty, very pretty young lady was watching them. "Lieutenant I can't help but notice that older gentleman. Do you know him?"

"Aye Sir, but I know the lady much better." Robert to the surprise of everyone asked John Hicks to invite the gentleman to join them. As he came over he gave a nod to the Lieutenant and introduced himself to Robert. "I am William Shaddock master of that two-masted snow the *Maryann* anchored below the fort." Robert responded, "I am Captain Robert Burnes the new commander of the sea fencibles for the Devon coast." The Lieutenant excused himself and went over to visit the young lady. Master Shaddock watched him. "The only thing I have besides my ship is my daughter.

I've done the best I could after her mother died. That there young officer better do right by her or there will be hell to pay." Robert purchased ale for the Master.

Hicks excused himself realizing that the Captain had his hands full at the moment. Robert asked, "Mr. Maxfield would you kindly introduce me to your young lady." She curtsied to the Captain and Maxfield made the introduction. "Sir this is Miss Margret Shaddock." As they finished their ale Robert told Master Shaddock that he would be at headquarters regularly and hoped to see him again. As he left Robert commented to Maxfield. "Watch yourself. Master Shaddock is no man to cross and I do not want to look for your replacement." The only reply was, "Aye Sir. See you in the morning."

At muster on Friday 132 men signed in. Word had gotten out that the new Captain was here. Yeoman Gosport reported only six men were absent. Captain Burnes read his orders to his new command. Maxfield drilled the men well. He was a serious and conscientious officer. Later that day the Lieutenant of the press-gang introduced himself. He was not a popular man in the area and he slept with one eye open.

At the end of the drill, Robert praised his young Lieutenant. He told him to stay in contact with him through his home in Riverton. He was going to step things up a bit and would have a plan by the next muster. Maxfield asked if he would be attending the next muster? Robert smiled. "Mr. Maxfield you have done well with no direction. I intend to provide help. However please be careful with the lady. I believe she is a keeper as the fishermen say." Robert and Mr. Hicks headed for home.

AN EYE FOR THE LADY

End of the second Dog Watch

Tom Davies had been footloose and fancy-free since arriving in Riverton. Molly the barmaid and waitress had worked at the Tally Ho for ten years. She had arrived in Riverton with her new husband who got a job at the woolen mill. As the villagers would say, the marriage did not take and he left her high and dry. Aunt Betty feeling sorry for her gave her a job and a room at the back of the inn.

If she had gentlemen suitors no one knows. Mr. Davies had become a fixture at the Tally Ho and was respected by everyone. He was forever tied to the fate of Captain Sir Robert Burnes. He was not a ladies man, but a relationship was struck between the two. After a while, the folks just took it for granted that Molly was Davies gal.

The arrival of John Hicks had changed the equation. John and Tom bunked together and now there was a void in the intimate relationship. Tom missed it. Molly missed it more. They did not know what to do. There comes a time in every relationship where it blossoms or dies. They were at that point.

It was Friday night at the Tally Ho. All the locals and the people who were staying at the inn were enjoying the ale and friendliness of the crowd. Molly was tending to the customers and Davies was at his usual place at the bar. One of the customers was seeking Molly's attention. It had happened a hundred times in the past, but Tom always shrugged it off. This time it was different. The victim made a big mistake and put his hand where it was not wanted. Davies was back on the *Kazidor* and the man never had a chance. Davies beat him to a pulp. Uncle George pulled him off the poor man before he lost his life. Davies looked to Molly, "You are all I want in life and I will share you with no man." Molly started to cry. He had actually said the words for the first time. Everyone who knew them started to applaud the couple as they hugged. Davies who always kept his emotions in check thought to himself, "What the hell just happened?" Sometimes the tide and wind are in harmony and the sailing is spectacular. A bridge had been crossed.

They both felt wonderful. Davies said, "I love you with all my heart." Now he was committed. He must speak to the Captain.

Robert arrived home from his trip to the sea fencibles Saturday morning. As he got down from the coach Davies asked, "I need to speak to you, Sir!"

"Of course. Let me get settled and greet Catherine. Come up to the cottage in about an hour and we will share a pot of coffee and biscuits if Rosie has some."

Davies, hat in hand, looking as somber as he ever had joined Robert for coffee. "I judge there is a grave issue. I hope you have not killed anyone."

"Oh no Sir. Well almost!" Robert did not know what to say. Davies continued, "It is worse than that. I am in love." How could such wonderful news be so somber? "Tom, can I assume we are talking about Molly?"

"Aye Sir! We are." Robert was happy. Tom had finally reached the proper conclusion "Well I give you joy Tom Davies. You two have been together almost from the time we came to the valley."

"Yes Sir. I am not sure what to do next. It is all so sudden. We need to find a place to live.

We can't live over the stable. This is a big step for me."

"Let me see if I understand this. You have been chasing this prize for a long time. You have achieved the weather gage. The prize is there for the taking. Board the prize and strike the colors. You boarded the *Kazidor* outnumbered two to one and fearlessly pushed forward, but you are hesitant against a single strawberry blond lady." He laughed. "All these details will work themselves out. I am happy for you Tom. She is a good person. You will be very happy. We all must anchor in our home port someday." At this point, Catherine came home. "What are you gentlemen about?"

"Tom and Molly have decided to tie the knot." Catherine matter of fact said, "It is about time Tom Davies. You and Molly have been together a long time." Davies confused said, "I thought it was a secret!" Catherine laughed. "Really if it was it is the worst kept secret in the village." Catherine now started planning. "We must get this moved along as my husband says waist not a minute." Davies sat there speechless.

EIGHTY HECTARES OF LAND

End of the Forenoon watch

Mr. Hancock invited his son in law Robert to his working luncheon with his friends Lord Eastman and the old Colonel. As he entered the study the magistrate and a local barrister were also in attendance. Jeffries offered a coffee to Robert. Mr. Hancock stated, "Shall we begin. Robert, we have a surprise for you. We have been discussing that now as a man of peerage you must have some holdings as the rest of the Lords in the valley do. Lord Eastman and I own two parcels adjacent to your land which runs along the brook behind the smithy. Mine is thirty hectares which have a small unoccupied cottage along the brook and a leasehold with a house that is being farmed. It is good bottomland. The family has been on the land for two generations. He does pay his rent most of the time, but has yet to yield a profit."

Lord Eastman then took over. "I have the adjoining fifty hectares. There is very little land suitable for planting. The rest is a very rocky hillside. My game-keeper's son is currently occupying the residence. He married one of the local girls, but so far has yielded me no income."

Robert was surprised by the offer. "How much would you require?" Mr. Hancock now started the negotiations. "Well, Robert we are not offering you a going enterprise. In fact, these properties are not yielding any income. We have been trying to sell them, but have had no offers. We think the best option would be to add them to your holdings. The whole would be more valuable than the parts." He smiled. "We are prepared to offer you a nonnegotiable price of one pound per holding." They all sat back in laughter. Lord Eastman stated." We have just made you an offer that no gentleman of peerage could refuse." Robert was speechless. Lambert told him to just sign. Then they all toasted the new landlord with one of Lambert's finest ports and went into lunch. After lunch, Lambert asked Robert, "If you are not busy would you mind accompanying me on my weekly walk-through of all the manufactories?" Robert was delighted.

They first went to the woodworking factory. Robert was fascinated with all the belts running from the water wheel shaft to the machines shaping wood. It was most impressive.

Next, they went to the tannery. The smell was horrendous. The piss cart had just arrived from collecting the village's daily output. This was used as the chemical acid to soften the hides.

Lambert told him this was his most profitable venture so far. He sold the tanned leather to cobblers and belt makers as far away as Plymouth.

The next stop was the woolen mill. It was a very labor intensive process which Mr. Handcock was automating to increase production. He had invested heavily in Hargraves spinning jennys to expand production. They were just setting up to receive the latest sheering from the sheepherders of the valley. It was a very seasonal business. Robert asked him what sheep yielded the most prized wool? "Suffolk was a dense fleece. Dorset was white with a finer fleece good for wool cloth." Robert thought, "Interesting."

The paper mill was next on the list. This was also a very smelly process but gave many of the lower class folks an opportunity to make money by selling wood chips collected from the surrounding valley. Lambert explained, "Our major customer is the newspaper broadsheets. It is a low-grade paper not suitable for writing." Robert watched as they sized the paper and cut off the excess. He asked, "What do you do with the trimmings?"

"We burn it, sir." Robert's mind was thinking. "Most people use the old newspaper to wipe themselves. Would it not be usable if you rolled it up and tied it with a piece of twine and sell it as necessary paper?" Lambert and his superintendent looked at each other. "What a splendid idea."

They then went to the brickworks which was a simple process of mixing the clay and sand with straw and water and setting it in molds, letting it dry, and then fire them for strength. Most of the village homes had been built from these bricks. Robert had another idea. "Could pipe be made from this process? Make each half in a mold and then use mortar to bind the two together. It sure would be better than the wood pipe they are currently using." Lambert looked to his foreman who said, "I will get right on it Mr. Hancock." Lambert was amazed that his son in law with his practical and logical mind could see things more simply than those who worked day to day with the product.

Lambert did not visit the nine coal bins that were located all around the valley. He said it was a simple business where he made a little profit off of each bucket of coal sold, but made a fortune off the volume of black gold used.

He commented to Abigail that evening over dinner that Robert had a great mind that was underutilized as a sea captain. Lambert then and there decided that the family business would rest on Robert's shoulders after Lambert's days were over.

That night at Blackstone Cottage the couple was in close contact in the bedchamber when Robert explained about the gift of property they had received. Catherine of course already knew from her mother what was going to happen. She was surprised by Robert's enthusiasm for her father's businesses.

The next day Robert with Catherine at his side were at the smithy early. "Good morning Tom." He was surprised to see them. Catherine went to the Tally Ho to ask Molly to join them. As they returned Robert asked the group to follow him up the path behind the smithy and paddock. The brook was running swiftly. It was very picturesque. As they rounded the corner, there was the cottage. Davies asked, "What is all this about?" Robert smiled, held Catherine's hand, and said to Molly and Tom, "Here is your new home." It was a thatched roof three-room affair, but very quaint. Tom and Molly were all smiles. Molly started to cry. Catherine held them both. "It is our wedding gift to you." Words could never explain the emotion of that moment!

THE FAILING BUSINESS

Six Bells in the Afternoon Watch

The ladies were having tea and Lambert and Robert were in the study. The Hancocks were getting ready for their trip North. Robert asked if there was anything he could do to assist while they were away. Lambert was very comfortable confiding in Robert. "I have a business in Winsford that is puzzling me. Elizabeth's husband George is overseeing the operation since it is closer to Great Torrington than here. It is losing money and I can not figure out why. George is in London with his father the Viscount. Now would be an opportune time to see what is wrong with the business. You seem to have an eye for looking at things from a different point of view. I will give you a letter of authorization to review the business as you see fit." Robert said, "I would be delighted to investigate. Thank you for your confidence."

They went to join the ladies and their tea. The twins were starting to show their condition. Both were babbling on about themselves. It was hard for Catherine to put up with their nonsense.

Victoria addressed her father. "Elizabeth and I have been meaning to ask you for a favor father." She looked to Catherine, "This pertains to you also." Abigail sensing that Lambert was about to be put on the spot asked, "Is this something that can be held until after our return?" Elizabeth said, "Mother we are in desperate need." Both spoke as one. "We need an increase in our allowance. We can barely get by on the £10 a month you give us." Lambert looked to Catherine. "She was crushed by what she heard. Her father was paying her £6 per month to teach the children of the village and her sisters were getting a £10 allowance for doing nothing. Lambert could see she was deeply hurt. Robert went to her side. He saw a way out of this. He smiled at his wonderful wife and said, "Sir, I think it is time that your children stood on their own two feet.

Ladies, you are both married to the two richest families in the valley. Catherine and I are well enough. I think it is time to cut the ties so to speak." The twins were outraged. Catherine just smiled. Lambert thought to himself, "Very well played." Then spoke, "Well said Robert. Yes ladies I believe it is time for all three of you to stand on your own." Abigail thought, "It has finally happened." The fluff head goddesses plan had completely collapsed. They drank their tea in silence. As they were leaving Lambert wanted to make amends to his favorite daughter.

Catherine spoke first. "Father, I am grateful for all I have. I am married to a wonderful man. I have a beautiful home, thanks to you. Robert and I have found our own way in life. I feel sorry for my sisters. They are missing so much in life by not having to work for it or appreciate all we have thanks to you and mother. We are blessed." She laughed. "Robert has a way of always finding a fair wind. She gave her father a kiss. "Enjoy your trip North to the family." Robert joined her and they both walked arm in arm home. They had the weather gage again.

Lambert and Abigail left for their trip North. Aunt Mimmie was staying at the residence to oversee the staff. Robert wanted to make the trip to Winsford. He asked Tom Davies and John Hicks to join him. Catherine wondered why Robert needed the boys. There couldn't possibly be trouble at father's factory or could there be? She bid a safe trip and they were on their way.

They took a public coach that made a stop in Winsford. Robert briefed them on their role. Mr. Davies was to play a separate part. Mr. Hicks and Sir Robert would look into the business. They arrived in Winsford. Davies went his separate way. They found the business on a side street. It was called Higley and Moore. They went into the office. "Good afternoon.

I am Mr. Burnes. This is Mr. Hicks. We are here to review the business for possible purchase." The man looking rather surprised said, "I am Mr. Manning. I run the day to day operations here." Robert replied, "Oh I was told to look for George Blyth."

"His Lordship is in London; perhaps you could come back when he returns."

"That would not be possible as this business is being offered for quick sale by the owner Mr. Lambert Hancock. We would like to look at the business and review the books today. Here is a letter from Mr. Hancock authorizing your full cooperation. Mr. Hicks, if you would start on this year's and last year's books, I will look over the factory." Robert went to the shop floor. Mr. Hicks sat at the desk and asked for the books. Robert found the foreman and got a tour of the manufacturing area. The man had worked here for over ten years and was very proud of his work. Robert learned that production had increased three years in a row. Robert asked about the coal business and was advised that Mr. Manning took control of that end of the business when George Blyth fired the bookkeeper and hired Manning. They spent most of the afternoon looking at the operation until Manning asked Robert to leave the foreman to his work. Mr. Hicks was busy in the office. He was very familiar with a ship's pursuer, who hid items and fudged numbers although in Manning's presents he pretended not to know.

Davies was in more familiar surroundings and had a seat in the local pub with ale in hand. Under his coat was Sir Robert's pocket pistol. He was wearing his best man-of-war look and inquiring about George Blyth and debts.

The barmaid who found Davies easy to talk to (no surprise) said, "The man you want to talk to would be in anytime and Georgie was well known in this establishment." Davies found this all interesting. A very large man came in and the barmaid nodded to him. The man looking like the gates to hell talked to the man behind the counter, looked over to Davies, and started to approach. Davies thought, "Oh boy here we go." The man sizing Davies up said, "Whats yous be looking for his lordship for?" Davies answered, "He owes my employer a lot of money." The man laughed. "Well stand in line May-tee. He owes me and a number of locals a considerable sum. He is very unlucky at cards. He has the disease. Rumor has it that he is in debt a considerable sum up in London. His father is Viscount Torrington, a big man in these parts. So he is good for the money. Good luck getting it. He and his man Manning have a scheme going on here so he is keeping up with his payments, but can't help himself if you knows what I mean. I would not hang around long in these parts if I was you." Davies drank his ale, winked at the barmaid, and without a word was out the door.

He headed for the inn to get a room and wait for the Captain. He and John Hicks arrived and took a table in the back of the dinner room. Robert had invited the foreman for dinner. The man arrived with the old bookkeeper in tow. They had a most interesting conversation. Daves, on full alert, was at the bar watching for trouble. After the meeting, Robert had a full picture of what was going on. That night Davies gave him the rundown on the gambling issues. "Mr. Hicks first thing in the morning you will find the Magistrate and bring him to the factory. Tom, you and I will deal with Manning."

"Aye Sir. We will."

At first light, they were in motion. The foreman and the old clerk were waiting at the front door. The Magistrate arrived soon after. They waited inside for Mr. Manning's arrival. He did not come and Mr. Hicks noticed that his personal effects were gone. The foreman gave the address where he had a room. Quick as a flash Davies was out the door.

Robert presented the letter from Mr. Hancock to the magistrate and introduced himself as Captain Sir Robert Burnes son in law of Mr. Hancock. John Hicks had the books out and was showing the Magistrate the errors he had found. A half-hour later Davies was back. "Sir, the scoundrel is gone. He cleared out his room and took the night coach up the coast." Robert's only reply was "Damn." The foreman showed where the cash was kept. It was empty. Robert told the Magistrate he would sign a warrant for his arrest. They pried open Sir George's desk and found another ledger with all the cash payments made by customers. Robert acclaimed, "So that is how he is doing it." Rather than pay an invoice they were getting discounted cash payments and not showing it as a sale on the books. "Crafty buggers" was Roberts' only comment.

Robert rehired the clerk and gave him a five-pound note for his help. The foreman would now be in charge until Mr. Hancock's return. He alerted the Magistrate to be sure that the business was not compromised by any of those low life's. He bid them all a good day and headed for the next coach home. The mystery had been solved. Now he had to protect Lambert from the revenge Viscount Torrington could bring on the family. Back to Riverton and real life.

TIE THE KNOT

Eight Bells in the Forenoon watch

While the gentlemen were in Winsford the ladies decided to move the wedding preparations along. Of course, everything including the ceremony, dinner, and party would happen at the Tally Ho where the couple had met. Uncle George ordered a few extra barrels of ale for the occasion. The whole village would be there. They got the Magistrate to agree to officiate. Next Friday would be the date. Catherine asked a few of her father's tradesmen to help fix up the cottage.

Molly was grateful for all that was done. Aunt Betty hunted around the village for furnishings.

When the men got off the coach Molly was there to greet Tom with the good news. Mr Hicks smiled because he could see the nervousness on his friend's face. He was going to call him "Cold feet Tom".

Mimmie and Aunt Betty found the wonderful dress and with a needle in hand were making it a perfect fit.

It was going to be the social event of the village. Tom Davies became very silent about the whole thing. The whole village was in a countdown with him. "Two days and a wakeup, Ah Tom." Robert was thinking that Tom was looking at it like ships punishment at the grating.

That fateful morning at first light Robert, John, and Tom were having their morning coffee and smoke at the smithy. Tom looking at his friends said, "Is it always like this? I have dreamed my whole life of having a wife. Now here it is right before me." John answered, "She is a good woman and no man should live alone." Robert looked to Tom, "As a captain going into action you always have a hesitation in the back of your mind. What if I fail? More importantly, what if I win. Life has brought you to this point and the only way is forward." Tom smiled, "Aye it is time. It is the right place and the right woman. I will strike my colors and surrender to my new life. I am ready." Robert replied, "Thank God Tom. You had us worried."

In the late afternoon, they all gathered at the Tally Ho to celebrate the union of two of their own: Tom and Molly. The Magistrate conducted the service like he was in a courtroom but with much more cheer. They said their vows with real meaning. They kissed. Then all hell broke out. It was the celebration of a lifetime.

They had roast beef, bread and ale. What could be better. Robert and Catherine were in the middle of it all. These were their friends and neighbors. This was their village and their home. Molly and Tom were more than friends. They were family. It was a happy time. While the groom could still stand Catherine and Robert lead the procession of the whole village up to the bride and groom's new home. The couple stood by the door as the whole village sang to them. Then bid them good night. Two bells in the second dog watch and all is well.

SEA FENCIBLES PART II

Two Bells in the Afternoon Watch

Robert had enlisted the help of the good Colonel to get the perspective of a military ground commander. They had borrowed Lord Eastman's smaller coach. The Colonel had jumped at the chance to wear his dress uniform and advise Robert on military matters. He had obtained an up to date map of the coast. They were taking the coast road looking for the most probable landing sites for French forces. Much of the coast is high cliffs and strong surf. They were eliminated.

The towns right on the coast were eliminated because of good roads for English forces to use. They picked three probable sites that were remote and had beach or river access. The good Colonel had an enjoyable three days with Robert. He took Lord Eastman's coach and headed home. Robert and Mr. Hicks headed for Plymouth. They heard there was a new Port Admiral to meet.

They arrived in Plymouth by public coach. Mr. Hicks went to obtain a room at the inn. Robert went to introduce himself to the Admiral. The secretary asked if he had an appointment? "No, I am Captain Burnes of the sea fencibles."

"Just a moment. I will see if Admiral Grayson has time for you." Robert could not believe his ears. It was his old squadron commander. It is a small world. The Admiral was at the door with a big smile on his face. "Welcome, Sir Robert. I told you our paths would cross again. I only hoisted my pennant three days ago."

"Yes Sir. News travels fast on the Devon coast."

"My schedule is full for the rest of the day. Could we dine together this evening? We have lots to discuss."

"I am at your disposal, Sir."

That night at dinner Robert learned of the surrender of the frigate *HMS Lightning* and the treachery of Commander Nibley. The Admiralty was keeping it very quiet, but a letter signed by all the officers in captivity was asking for his Court Martial. The French would soon let it be known to all the London papers. Robert was shocked. "Admiral Howe's grandson was murdered and the *Lightning* was captured without a fight. It is a black day for the Royal Navy Sir." The Admiral said, "I warned the First Lord, but he was more interested in pleasing Lord Nibley." They then turned their discussion to the days in Antigua and life at home. After they drank to the King, Admiral Grayson asked, "How can I help you, Captain Burnes?" Robert outlined his new plan for the defense of the Devon coast. Admiral Grayson advised that he would see what he could do and send supplies to Exmouth. He laughed at the idea of firing those old cannons, but he would send a Master Gunner with equipment to try. He also told Robert that the government was quietly negotiating with the French for peace at the moment. Robert stated that he would stop to pay a courtesy call from time to time. Grayson told him, "I hope that I will be able to use your skills at some point in the future."

"I am at your service whenever you need me Sir, but for the time being the defense of the Devon coast has my full attention." The Admiral laughed and said, "Good luck with that Sir Robert."

Robert and Hicks were off to Exmouth to attend the next muster. Robert had formulated a plan. "Let's be at em Mr. Hicks." They arrived on Thursday. Lieutenant Maxfield was there with Yeoman Gosport. Robert laid out his map and put forth his plan. "I have viewed the coastline all week and much of it is high bluff or cliffs. The surf will also make much of the coast undesirable for the French. I also think they will stay away from towns and populated areas. Based on this I have identified three probable landing sites, Teignmouth on the river Teign, the beaches at Torcross, and of course Exmouth. There is also Blackpool, which I believe the locals call Smugglers Cove." Lieutenant Maxfield seemed uneasy when he mentioned Smugglers Cove. "Mr. Maxfield I would like you to make up three watch bills: A Larboard, Starboard, and a Command section. Appoint a Boatswain for each group. Have it ready for the muster."

As the muster was formed Friday morning Robert asked, "Mr. Gosport how many are present?" "All 138 present for duty. Sir." Robert asked, "The six men who missed last muster, I wish to see them in the building immediately." The six names were called and as they walked into the office they looked to Lieutenant Maxfield who followed. Robert told him to return to the muster. He faced the six men and asked why they missed the last muster. The spokesman said, "We are fishermen Sir and must feed our families. It won't happen again." Captain Burnes suspected other motivations. "Gentlemen you have very much the look of sailors, but I doubt very much you are humble fishermen. In fact, you sir (the spokesman for the group) look very much like a man I saw at the helm of a thirty-six foot cutter which was heading to sea as I crossed the river on my first trip here. I am not in the Revenue Service. I am in the King's Royal Navy responsible for guarding the coast. If you miss muster again I will see you pressed into the Kings service. Do I make myself clear!" They all responded "Aye Sir." Robert now had their attention. "I know your trade and there is not anything that happens on this coast that you are not aware of. If there is any French activity at all you will bring it to me!" The leader said, "Aye Sir. Understood."

"One more thing. Do not involve Lieutenant Maxfield in your endeavors. That is all. Return to your divisions." As they left Robert thought "One more piece of the puzzle falls into place. We will now have good intelligence on French activity."

The Master Gunner arrived by wagon midday with all the tools of his trade. He reported to Robert. "Sir, Are those the cannon you wish me to inspect? I believe my grandfather was alive the last time they were fired!" At Robert's direction, he took the wagon over to the wall next to the guns.

Training had stopped and all eyes were on the guns. The Captain, Lieutenant Maxfield, and three men he had designated as gunners assisted the Master Gunner. He looked down the barrel of the first two with a candle in hand and shook his head. "These barrels are pitted stem to stern Sir." He looked down the third barrel and looked down again. He then took a rammer and inserted it a foot before it stopped. Next he took an iron bar and hammered it. Everyone on the field expected to hear an explosion. There was none. He then inspected the forth barrel and presented his finding to the good Captain. "Sir we may be in luck with the number three gun.

The rest are no good for anything. There is a cannonball lodged in the mouth of the third gun and may have prevented pitting from occurring." Robert with all eyes on him said, "Splendid let's see if we can get the ball out." The Gunner said, "It has been lodged there fifty years and more." Robert with his expert eye for the gun said, "I have an idea."

Lieutenant Maxfield moved everyone back. Robert and the Gunner with a boring tool opened up the touch hole and poured as much fine powder into the cannon as they could. With a stick, they pushed through the touch hole and moved as much powder as they could and added more. It was a nerve-racking moment. They put a slow match down the hole and lit it. They moved away as fast as they could. All eyes were on the gun. A minute went by and nothing happened. All the men started to laugh except Robert and the Gunner. They continued to watch the gun and the mouth of the river. There was a tremendous explosion. Many of the men dove for cover. The cannon was obscured by smoke. Robert and the Gunner watched the bay. There was a splash. Robert commented, "I estimate about 250 yards." The Gunner said, "Aye Sir, and that was with about half a charge." He then went to sponge out the barrel and inspect the gun. The three volunteers went with him. He started his instructions on loading.

Robert looked to the men with a smile. "Mr. Maxfield let us return to duty. Take ten men and go to the armory and pick out four or five good rounds and have the men start chipping the rust off of them."

At this point, most of the town's people were coming to the fortress to see what was happening. It was the talk of the town. The Master Gunner reported, "Sir I believe you have a serviceable piece." Robert answered, "Very good. Well done. Now let's get training the gun crew. Mr. Maxfield, please get the three divisions back to work." The rest of the day went well. The new gun crew fired twice more and moved the powder and supplies to the armory.

They were having dinner at the inn. Robert invited Master Shaddock, his daughter, and the good Lieutenant. Shaddock matter of fact said, "I here you have sniffed out our local smuggling coves." Robert nodded. "Why sir whatever do you mean. Smuggling is a part of this coast this last century and I suspect it will go on long into this century. As long as it does not interfere with my mission here, I have no interest in it. Mr. Maxfield and I are Kings officers and will follow our orders," as he looked to the young Lieutenant.

Robert changed the subject. "Mr Shaddock have you carried coal in your ship." Shaddock replied, "Aye Captain. It is a lucrative cargo in these parts. I have tried many ports on the Northside of Bristol Bay, but without a contract, you only get the overflow. It is a very hazardous journey in the winter months. Most of the coal goes up the Exe through here and Exeter.

Nothing moves without the approval of a man called Hancock who lives in your parts. Do you know him?" Robert smiled. "I am acquainted with him." They completed their dinner. The Lieutenant and his lady had time together. It would be off to home in the morning.

THE COTTAGE AND HOME

Six Bells in the Forenoon Watch

Robert and Mr. Hicks arrived home Monday morning. Tom Davies met them. "Sir, the Magistrate has been inquiring about your return. There is a box at your door. A sailor from Exmouth delivered it this morning." Robert asked John Hicks to advise the Magistrate he was home. He headed for the cottage after two weeks away from home. Rosie greeted him." Welcome home Sir. Lady Catherine is teaching the children. Miss Mimmie is still at the Hancock residence. The mail is on the table. Is there anything I can get you?" Robert replied, "Some coffee and your biscuits if you have some."

He stared at the box at the door. He suspected what it was. He opened it to find six bottles of fine French brandy. There was no note, but he knew who it was from. Rosie arrived with the coffee. In his mail was a letter from his agent. It was the news he expected. Mr. Waterhouse had discreetly checked on young Sir George's gambling in London. The letter confirmed that he owed large sums to two gambling establishments in the city. He also gave him an accounting of his prize funds which now totaled almost £4,000. He was not rich but very comfortable with this and his bonds at Childs and Company. He had a very quiet and enjoyable morning. He put the brandy in the sideboard and waited for the Magistrate's arrival.

Mr. Hicks escorted him to the house. "Good morning Sir Robert. We have much to discuss. People are still being moved off the land as the Lords of the valley proceeded with the enclosure. The younger ones which the magistrate described as "young ruffians" were now organizing and holding meetings in the old building by the river. This place was known as the sick house during the smallpox epidemic.

It was never occupied after that. All the people who died were buried in one mass grave there. Robert's mother was among them. "They are talking about sedition Sir Robert. They want to overthrow the King and take the land from the Lords of the valley. It is anarchy, Sir," Robert knew that something had to be done, but what? Many of the older group were neighbors and citizens of the village. The Lords had legal rights to do as they pleased with their land, but there had to be some accommodation for the people. They were the real England, not the Lords. "Sir Robert, many of the Lords are calling for the dragoon's to come and hang the lot of them." Robert responded, "Good God. These are our neighbors or their children. There must be another solution. Allow me to look into it." The Magistrate asked for John Hicks's services. He had many legal documents that needed copying. Robert then had another idea. "Could you check discreetly and see if there are any encumbrances on the Torrington estate." They parted and Robert changed into work clothes and went to the smithy to talk to Davies.

While having a smoke with Davies, he confirmed that the village was in turmoil and many of the young folk were asking for work. Any kind of work. Davies' comment was, "This is not going to end well Sir. The people feel ill-used and the Lords of the valley don't care." There was no easy solution, but a solution nonetheless must be found.

Catherine came home to the waiting arms of Robert. Catherine advised Rosie that dinner would not be required and that she could have the rest of the day off.

Lady and Lord retired to the bed chamber for a much-needed reunion. Sailing full and bye.

THE DINNER

Six bells in the afternoon watch

Lambert and Abigail had returned from their trip North and invited the whole family to dinner to celebrate their return. Robert had just returned from a week with his sea fencibles detachment and had been looking forward to his Friday night with the boys at the Tally Ho. One frown from Catherine and Robert decided there was always next week. They were both dressed to the nines. Robert had on his dress uniform. Catherine had her bobble (Ruby) on full display.

The fluff head goddess's we're playing up the fact that they were both with child. It was a pleasant afternoon and the young Lords kept their mouths in check. Of course Lord Eastman and the old colonel were invited. Lambert seemed to be in a very happy mood. They all took their places at dinner and

Lambert began with a toast. "We had a most excellent trip and enjoyable time with the rest of the Hancock family, but it is good to be back home. To the family." Here, here.

After the first reveal both Victoria and Elizabeth commented, "Catherine you should realize that the clock is ticking and being older you should keep that in mind." Catherine just smiled. Robert came to her rescue. "Well ladies this is not all on Catherine. I believe I have a small part to play. Being at sea makes it most difficult, but I shall endeavor to do my part." This brought laughter from the whole group. The young Lords were on their best behavior and it was a very pleasant dinner.

After dinner the ladies retired to the parlor and the men produced their smokes to enjoy with a great bottle of brandy. Robert asked, "Sir George (Elizabeth's husband) the bottle stands by you. Would you pass it along?" This seemed to irritate the young Lord. "By all means" as he passed the bottle.

Lambert announced. "I have very good news gentlemen. The heavy rains this winter have caused a major slide on a mountain on one of the Hancock family holdings. It has revealed a major coal seam which looks very promising. As luck would have it I am next in line to develop this opportunity. Now it is in a remote area and is going to take a consider-able amount of money to develop." Both young Lords stepped in. "We give you joy, father Lambert. Well done." Robert continued to listen. Lambert explained. "It is going to take £10,000 to get this operation going.

So I am giving you gentlemen the opportunity to invest in this venture. I am sure if the seam is as deep as we think, it could yield at least ten times your investment. I can put together about £5,000 and Lord Eastman is pledging £2,000. I am offering each of my son-in-laws the opportunity to invest £1,000 and become a ten percent partner in the enterprise." Robert without hesitation said, "Thank you for letting us in on the venture. Count me in. How soon do you need the funds?" Lambert smiled. "You are very welcome Robert."

He looked to the young Lords who were both very silent. Lord Ransom spoke first. "My father, with enclosure, is expanding his planting on the estate and I do not have any excess funds at the moment." Then Lord Torrington spoke. "I don't have those kinds of funds. I will speak to my father, perhaps he would be interested." Lambert's quick response was "NO! This is for the family only." Lord Ransom had an idea. "Father Lambert could you possibly loan us the money and we could pay you back with the profits?" Lambert was very disappointed in them both. "If I had those kinds of funds I would not be offering this bird in hand. I wish no bank to be involved. They are vultures to any business enterprise." He then gave them a word of advice. "Why don't both of you gentlemen curtail your season in London. Both my daughters would do well to stay home with children on the way. That should give you the funds to invest." Both were outraged by the request. How dare their father in law tell men of peerage how to live their lives.

Lambert had handed them a great opportunity and they shoved it back in his face. Robert realized that this conversation was going very wrong. He interrupted, "Excuse me." He asked Jeffries the butler, "Would you be so kind as to ask Lady Catherine to join us for a moment. She came in smiling. "What can I do for my husband?" Robert explained. "Your father has offered us a tremendous opportunity to invest in one of his coal enterprises. I want you to be aware it will involve much of our finances." Catherine put both her hands on her husband's shoulders and replied. "If the two men I admire most in the world, my father and my husband join in a venture it would surely have my blessing." She winked at her father and returned to the ladies. Robert looked to Lambert. "£3,000 count us in and thank you." The young Lords, who still felt ill-used, could not let it go. Lord Torrington spoke. "Burnes, you astound me. You ask your wife's permission to spend money! You live in that little worker's cottage and have £3,000 in the bank. What are you thinking? You have joined the peerage class." Robert thought these two are worthless. "Catherine and I have a special relationship and we live very comfortably and need not flaunt our wealth, such as it is. I honor father Hancock that he would include us." The conversation was at an end.

The Ladies came back in for dessert and tea. Abigail sensed that the mood had changed. Lambert was very somber. After desert, the young Lords made their excuses, formally thanked Abigail and Lambert, and made their exit.

After they left, in Lord Eastmans' presents, Lambert with Abigail at his side told the happy couple that he was blessed to have their support. "Catherine, Robert, you are my rock in this ever-changing world. I am so honored by your marriage and the support you have given me." They hugged to the point of embarrassment. Robert knew Lambert would need his support in the future. The other two-thirds of the family were going to be a problem.

THE BUSINESS LUNCHEON

Start of the Afternoon Watch

Lambert made Robert part of his weekly luncheon. Robert got there early and Jeffries escorted him to Mr. Hancock's study. Robert had his demand note from Lloyd's for £3,000 ready.

Lambert's barrister would be at the meeting. Robert stated, "Sir I think we should review my visit to Winsford before anyone gets here" Lambert said, "I assumed it was bad news since you did not bring it up at the dinner."

"Yes sir. It is a sad state of affairs. It is a very well run business but I am afraid Sir George was not looking out for your interests." Lambert felt bad. Robert laid out the whole issue of bringing Manning on board and the firing of his original clerk. Then Robert gave him the accounting book with all the discounted cash sales. "None of these sales were ever recorded on the company books." Lambert looked at it with amazement. "This is over £1,400. Dear lord. Why would he do this to me?" Robert exclaimed. "There is more. This man Manning ran the cash coal business in Winsford. I can't account for what the losses are there. I hope I have not overstepped Sir but I reinstated the old clerk and appointed the foreman who I think is a loyal employee to run the business. The magistrate was summoned and I filed a warrant for Manning's arrest. When he got wind of what we were about, he took all the cash in the cash box and left town." Lambert sat there speechless. He was mad. Why had this rich young Lord who is a member of the family done this to him? "I was attempting to bring him into my business." Robert had to be careful for he was on untested ground. "I did some checking while I was there and he has had an association with some very seedy characters. He has a gambling problem and owes many of the locals money. I believe he was desperate sir." Lambert still did not understand the full picture. "Why did he not go to his father?" Robert said, "I don't believe his father knows anything of the debt or the gambling problem. It goes further sir. Through my agent in London, I have learned that he is heavily in debt at two of the biggest gambling establishments in London. He also has borrowed money against the estate here in Riverton." Lambert said, "Dear God what do I do?" Robert had a plan. "I think that you tell him that his services are no longer needed, The business has been losing money for some time and you are going to sell it. Tell him that the manager Manning has an arrest warrant out for stealing cash from the business. He will think he has hidden his issues and will not say a word. Face will be saved and his large ego will not be hurt."

Lambert was relieved for the time being. "Thank you Robert this could have been devastating for the family." Robert was also relieved he did not want to be the source of problems for the family. Then he ended on a positive note. "After you have corrected the books it will show a sizable profit and you will be able to make money on the sale." Lambert laughed. "You have a fine head on your shoulders. It is wasted sailing ships for the Royal Navy. Thank you! Now let's wait for the others and get this coal mine in production." The agreement was signed. Lambert Hancock was Majority Partner with 50%.

Lord Eastman was a 20% Partner and Sir Robert Burnes was a 30% Partner. He was now in the coal business. The humble young man from Riverton had come a long way. He had much farther to go both in the Royal Navy and in life.

Life is full of surprises!

THE RITES OF SPRING

Six Bells in the Forenoon Watch

The Hancocks were holding their annual May Day celebrations. This was Viscount Torrington's first time at the event. Most of his holdings were on the other side of Devon in the town of Great Torrington. He arrived late with his son George and his beautiful wife Elizabeth. They went through the receiving line and George made the introductions. Lambert and Abigail welcomed their guest.

"It is an honor to have you here Lord Torrington." He had not seen any of the Hancocks since the wedding of his son to Elizabeth. George then introduced him to many of the guests and gave him the lay of the land so to speak. "That is my good friend Sir Kenneth Ransom." (Married to Hancock's other daughter Victoria who was as beautiful as Elizabeth).

His son had done very well in picking a wife. "That is lord Eastman. He holds the biggest estate in the valley, but his son is dead, so he has no heir. His estate will be available at some point in time. That is Burnes and his wife Catherine, Hancock's other daughter. He is a thorn in my side. He and his scarface wife have Hancock's ear and are causing me problems. That couple over there owns the local inn and are Burnes Aunt and Uncle. They are peasants really." George introduced his father to the Magistrate, the old Colonel, and many of the Lords and Ladies of the Valley. Lord Torrington thought, "This is a good place to make useful contacts. He wondered why George had not."

It was a delightful afternoon. The food and wine were superb. Hancock knew how to throw a party. Then, Abigail, Catherine, and Mimmie put on a splendid recital. He noticed that much of the group centered around the Naval Captain and his wife. She was wearing that splendid ruby necklace and that exquisite gown. He wondered how a naval officer could afford that. He wondered why George was not cultivating these people. He and his friend young Lord Ransom just stayed with their group rather than mingle with the other guests. He decided to have a private conversation with Hancock. They retired to his study. "Well, Hancock you certainly know how to throw a party."

"Thank you, My Lord" was the reply. The Viscount wanted to apply some pressure on behalf of his son.

"I understand from my son that he is no longer involved in your business in Winsford."

"Yes, I have sold the business." Lord Torrington responded, "Yes George told me that you had an employee that was stealing from the firm." Lambert knew he was on very perilous ground. He decided to let it go. "Perhaps George could gain experience with one of your other ventures?" Lambert could see that he was now trapped so he let him know, "I asked him and my other two sons in law to join a coal mining venture. Your Son declined."

"He did what!" was the Viscount's response. Lambert man of business was going to tell it like it was. "Yes, he was even quite insulting about it. To be honest with you Sir, I sold the business in Winsford to protect our family so that no scandal touched George or Elizabeth. The Viscount was getting very irritated at this point. "What are you saying Sir?" Lambert said, "Are you aware of your son's gambling problems?"

"I am not!" Lambert had to lay out the whole problem. "He owes a number of unscrupulous people money in Winsford and unfortunately the business became involved, so I sold it to avoid further embarrassment to the family. I also have it on good authority that he is indebted to gambling houses in London." The Viscount could not believe this. Lambert thought he might as well lay it all out. "Are you aware that he has encumbered his estate here in Riverton?" From the look on Lord Torrington's face, he could see he was not. "We both need to protect the family.

Elizabeth is with child and will hopefully give you an heir." They both sat quietly as Lambert poured some brandy. Now they could get to know each other.

The festivities had moved out on the terrace. It was a delightful afternoon. The two young Lords with the fluff head goddesses at their side were commenting that father Lambert was getting the facts of life in his study that all men of peerage were to be respected. Catherine and Robert were enjoying themselves when Robert sensed that something was wrong. The people were looking towards the forest at the back of the lawn. Young men were coming across the lawn shouting at the guests. Two or three of the ruffians were shouting insults as they approached the two young Lords. One had a knife in his hand. Sir George tripped and fell to the ground. The twins were screaming. Sir George was pleading, "Please no." The man went to stab him. A shot rang out. The man dropped the knife and fell backward. Captain Burnes, pocket pistol in hand moved toward the mob and drew his sword. The good Colonel was by his side with a sword drawn.

Back at the smithy Tom and John were enjoying a smoke when they heard the shot. Davies said, "trouble" then grabbed two cutlasses hanging on the wall. He gave one to John and at a dead run, they headed for Hancocks.

The guests were huddled on the terrace. Lambert and Viscount Torrington were now looking at the dying man and Sir George crying on the ground. Robert with a pistol in one hand sword in the other, joined by the Colonel, were standing on the lawn in front of the mob of twenty or so. From the side of the residence Tom and John, cutless at the ready, arrived. Robert gave the order. "Mr. Hicks to Larboard. Mr. Davies to Starboard. Ten feet apart. Let's drive this rabble into the woods." The mob quickly lost its nerve and dispersed.

The magistrate pronounced the man dead and put a tablecloth over the body. The group moved inside. Mr. Hicks and Mr. Davies stood guard on the Terrace. Lambert thanked Robert for his quick action. Viscount Torrington gave him a nod. Many of the guests were leaving. The Lords and officials of the valley retired to Lambert's study. The ladies remained in the parlor. The twins were quite disturbed by it all. Their protective bubble had burst.

In the study, Viscount Torrington was observing and watching who would take charge. Young Sir George had recovered his courage. "They should all be hanged." The others were calling for the dragoon's to be summoned. The magistrate was going to put out a warrant for their arrest by God. Lord Ransom stated. "This is an insult to the King and gentlemen of peerage and justice must be served."

Lambert asked, "Please settle down. Let's talk with reason here!" He looked to Sir Robert and nodded. Robert took a few seconds to look at the group then responded. "Gentlemen, we have brought this on ourselves. We have driven the people off the land with no thought to their well being. Did you think they would just quietly disappear? These are people who have lived and worked in Riverton and the valley for generations. If this is handled wrong the animosity toward the ruling class will grow. The dragoon's or warrants or even hanging will not solve this problem. If you will not stir the pot any further, I will solve this and the good people of Riverton will be on our side." Lambert then looked to the group. "Please a man has died. Let's have calmer heads prevail. I have trust in Sir Robert. Magistrate do you agree?" He nodded and left to take care of the body.

Viscount Torrington had his answer. Lambert Hancock and Captain Burnes were the force in this valley. Hancock did have the best interests of his family at heart and now he would have to deal with his son's issues.

Mr. Davies and Mr Hicks would stand guard for the rest of the evening. It had not been the best day for the valley.

PILLOW TALK

The Second Dog Watch

After the events of the day, Sir Robert and his lady retired to the bed-chamber. Tonight they would aggressively enjoy each other stirred by the events of the day. They had much to talk about before exhaustion overtook them. Catherine asked, "Do you feel bad about the man killed?" Robert responded, "I feel bad that it did not have to happen, but from my youngest days in the navy I learned to assess, react, and move on. We can't go back only forward. If Sir George had died I am not sure but the world would be better off. However, he did not deserve to die."

Catherine reflective stated, "There were some of my ex-students in that mob. Joshua Thornwell whose family was pushed off the Ransom Estate were sheep-herders. His father was lucky enough to get a job in the woolen mill. He was sweet on Amie Millet who married the gamekeeper's son who lives on our property. Her family had no options after being pushed off the land so she was given up for marriage at such a young age. They were both promising students."

"Fear not my love. We do what we can. I will end this. They will all be in the King's Service for better or worse."

"Oh, Robert is there no better way?"

"Well I started in that manner and so did Tom Davies and John Hicks."

"Yes but not all captains are like you. I just look at the marks on your back to remind me that a King's ship can be a brutal place."

"I can think of no better answer and if mob rule persists Riverton will not be a pleasant place to live. I wish you to be very careful until this is over, for if they can't get to me, they will seek a weaker target such as you my love. I will make Tom or John available to escort you until this is all over."

"Good night my noble protector."

"Pleasant dreams my lovely lady."

The village of Riverton slept, but the young radicals now had a martyr to help their cause. Man with no purpose or hope is a lost soul and the devil's handy work. Beat to Quarters lads. The ship is in peril!

THE PRESS GANG

Start of the First Dog Watch

The ruffians of the valley were getting more agitated and abusive to the locals who tried to avoid them. They held meetings at the old sick house and were planning their next move. Captain Burnes had Davies watching them. Tom Davies came up to the cottage. "Good morning Sir. I believe we have smoked them out. Friday next they will have an evening meeting and then they plan to disrupt the estates in the valley." Robert replied, "We will be ready. I have sent John to the sea fencibles to have Lieutenant Maxfield get the local press-gang ready. Mr. Hancock has loaned us two of his coal wagons. They are waiting in Exeter. I will send word for them to be on the South Road by late afternoon Friday." Davies replied with a laugh, "Aye Sir. I am afraid it will interfere with our Friday night at the Tally Ho."

"There is always next week Tom. Everything must look normal. Let's make sure the ladies are not out and about that afternoon or evening. I pray nothing happens between now and then."

Catherine came home from teaching the children. "The town is in turmoil. Even the children are asking what will happen!" Robert said, "Fear not my love it will all be over very soon." He was writing a dispatch to Admiral Grayson requesting a brig to be dispatched to Exmouth on Saturday to receive the pressed men. He gave it to the post rider heading for Exeter asking that it be sent to Plymouth post haste. It was urgent.

Robert went to his normal business luncheon at the Hancock's residence. He advised Lambert and Lord Eastman all was ready. "If you could stop any of the local Lords and landowners from any hasty action that could give the plan away it would be helpful." Lord Ransom was still making noise about bringing the dragoons to the village. Lambert promised to speak to him.

On Thursday Catherine was accosted by two of the thugs while coming home from teaching the children. Mr Davies dispatched the two of them and they ran away. Tensions were high!

Riverton was on edge.

Friday morning Robert escorted Catherine to school. The whole village watched. He then went to have coffee at the smithy with Davies. "All is well Sir.

I hope this plan works." Molly came down and gave lunch to the men. In the afternoon Robert went and escorted Catherine home. He put on his number one uniform, poured himself a brandy, and sat in the parlor waiting. The clock did not seem to move. He watched from the window as Davies closed up the smithy and walked down the road with his blacksmith bag. He bet Tom had his service pistol and cutlass in there.

As it approached twilight, Robert checked his pocket pistol, put on his Marine Saber, and walked down the path to the bridge. He could hear the crowd down at the sick house. The good Colonel in dress uniform approached. "Good evening Captain Burnes. All is in readiness?" Robert replied, "Aye, I can see the wagons coming up the road." Before they reached the house, ten men jumped out and surrounded the sick house. The Lieutenant of the press-gang was shouting orders. This was a payday for him as he got head money for each man he pressed. He could see Mr. Hicks and Mr. Davies directing the men. The Lieutenant at the top of his lungs shouted, "In the name of the King I hereby press you into the Royal Navy." The colonel commented, "So it begins." Lieutenant Maxfield approached and saluted. "Good evening Sir." Robert replied, "Right on time. Well done." The townspeople were coming into the street to watch. They now knew what was going on. Uncle George, Aunt Betty, Catherine, Mimmie, and Rosie joined them in front of the Tally Ho. A woman in the crowd was crying. She went to Catherine with an urgent appeal. "Please save my son. He is a good boy. I beg you Lady Catherine. Please speak to the Captain."

Catherine walked to her husband's side and in her most demure voice said, "That is Mrs. Thornwell crying, Robert. Her son is in that building." Robert looked to his lovely wife and in his best command voice said, "This is the King's business and there can be no exceptions." Catherine smiled. "The whole village is watching. You have never refused a request of mine. Please my love, for me!" Robert was powerless. "Lieutenant Maxfield, would you fetch Mr. Davies for me."

"Aye Sir." In a few minutes, Davies was at his side. "Tom, would you find Joshua Thornwell in that mob and bring him to me?" By now the press-gang had all the landsmen sorted and bound up. They were being loaded in the wagons. Lieutenant Maxfield approached. "Twenty-eight prime hands ready for transport Sir." Robert answered, "Very well, but I believe the count will be twenty-seven. Tell the Lieutenant of the press I will make up the head money on the one lad.

After this is done, have Mr Hicks bring you up to the cottage for some late supper. I will see you get a room at my uncle's inn. You can catch the coach in the morrow."

"Aye Sir thank you." Here came Mr Hicks and Mr. Davies with the young lad between them.

His parents stood next to Catherine. Robert in a very stern voice said, "You are Joshua Thornwell?"

"I am your Lordship." Robert responded, "I prefer Captain. I hereby release you from the press and into your parents custody. If I hear of any sedition or remarks against the King or the Lords of this valley, I will take you to Plymouth and place you on a ship myself. Is that clear!

Now go to your parents." Mrs. Thornwell, still crying said, "Oh thank you, Captain. God bless you. We will see that he respects the King." Off they went before the good Captain changed his mind. Catherine with a little courtesy smiled and said, "Thank you, kind Sir." Robert just shook his head. "I must be getting soft in my old age." He smiled back.

The wagons headed down the South Road toward Exmouth. The streets were cleared. Most of the menfolk went into the Tally Ho to have a wet. Robert asked Tom, John, and Lieutenant Maxfield to come up to the cottage for a late supper. Rosie would find something for them to eat.

All was well in the good village of Riverton and the valley returned to its quiet self.

SEA FENCIBLES PART III

End of the Afternoon Watch

The next muster for the sea fencibles was this weekend. He met Lieutenant Maxfield early and they went to the three possible landing sites along the coast to review the defense of each location. Robert, at Lord Eastman's insistence, took his small coach. They got to the last site at Blackpool late in the day. Before they got to the beach they noticed a small dwelling along the road and a number of men in uniform were at the building. Lieutenant Maxfield said, "Looks like men from the Revenue Service Sir." They had the coach stop before the beach and they got out to walk the hillside along the beach. There was a rocky cove at the end of the beach and a cutter that looked vaguely familiar was anchored off the point. Four men had pulled up in a boat. The two officers went to investigate. These men looked to the Captain.

"Good evening Sir." Robert said, "Gentlemen I hope you will not be late to muster tomorrow because the building at the head of the road is occupied by the revenue service."

"Back to the boat. Begging your pardon Sirs. If you will run off that way I will fire a shot and we will be out of here." The shot was fired. The Revenue Service came down the road to save the Royal Navy. The cutter and crew were gone. The two smiled all the way back to Exmouth.

When they arrived at the old fortress Sir Robert noticed that the *Maryann* was not at anchor. Maxfield explained that he had a cargo to deliver up the coast and would be home tomorrow. He showed the Captain the cottage he planned to rent below the fort next to the harbor. He explained, "It is two pounds per month, Sir. Margret loves it. She would not have to live on her father's ship."

"So you are ready to make the move. If you pay two pound for lodging that will only give you six pound to live on. Not an easy task Mr Maxfield."

"No Sir, but I am determined to make her my wife."

At the inn, there was the man who owned the property. He said, "Are you ready to sign Lieutenant?" The Captain jumped in. "Two pounds is a very steep price, Sir. Very steep indeed."

"Well, what are you proposing Lieutenant." Before he could answer Sir Robert said, "Two-year lease for thirty pounds." The man smiled and said, "Done." Sir

Robert paid the man. Mr. Maxfield signed. Sir Robert said, "Consider it a wedding present. Now that Miss Shaddock has a place to live, it should impress her father. All in all, it has been a very profitable two days wouldn't you say, Mr. Maxfield?"

"Aye Sir it has."

Muster the next day was a flurry of activity. The gun crew fired the old gun six times marking marker shots for future reference. The three teams were now organized and Lieutenant Maxfield with a map in hand was briefing each group on their assigned area to defend. Many people from the town of Exmouth watched each muster. It was a big event in this small town.

The leader of the smugglers asked to speak to Captain Burnes. He thanked him for the help on the beach the day before. Captain Burnes just wanted information. "What do you have for me in the way of French activity on the Devon coast!" Robert was startled by the information he got. A French Corvette and Brig were on the coast every three weeks or so. They were a letter of mark privateers not French National ships. The brig worked close inshore hoping to snap up coastal traders. The Corvette was there to cover for the brig and watch for bigger opportunities. He believed they would be back on the coast in seven days when the moon was at its darkest.

They were dropping people off or picking them up. He was not sure. The smugglers were staying home while the French were on the coast. Robert wasted no time in getting this information to Admiral Grayson.

After the muster was over they all went to the local inn to have a wet. Lieutenant Maxfield had arranged for dinner with the Shaddocks. He asked his Captain to join him for moral support. Master Shaddock was not in a happy mood. He sensed from his daughter that things were a miss. Robert asked, "How was your trip?" Shaddock replied, "Got it done but not very profitable." Master Shaddock was not pleasant. "We live by our witts here on the coast. Making a living on coastal trade was not for everyone." Robert said, "Yes for those with a coal contract the living is much more profitable."

"Aye Captain. That's the truth." Robert reached into his pocket and gave a letter to Master Shaddock. "What's this?" as he opened the letter. It was an authorization to carry coal from five different ports on the North coast of Bristol Bay for the Hancock Partnership. Robert looked at him. "I believe your ship has come in, so to speak, Master Shaddock."

"I'll be Damned. How did you arrange this? Do you know Hancock?" Robert looked at the young couple. "He is my father in law." It turned into a happy night. Ale was had by all. Then Shaddock said, "There must be a catch." Robert said, "Mr. Maxfield you have the floor." Before he could speak, Margert interrupted, "Papa, I can not live on your ship forever. I wish to live on land in a house of my own." Maxfield now with the courage to ask said, "I have obtained a lease on the cottage below the fortress. I am just a Lieutenant at the moment, but my prospects for advancement are good. I wish to make Margret my wife." There he had said it! Shaddock now realized that fateful day had come. "Well lad she is yours, but if you don't treat her right there will be hell to pay." The deed was done. Lieutenant Maxfield had his bride. Sir Robert Burnes had a small part to play. Now he was sure that his young Lieutenant would stand to his duty.

Master Shaddock and his young bride would see to it. Sailing full and Bye.

OFF TO LONDON

The Morning Watch

The good Captain felt good to be home. Tom Davies was there to greet him.

"How was Exmouth Sir?" Robert with a sense of humor said, "We saved the town for another month. No French insight." Tom said, "That sailor was here again. This time there are three boxes on your doorstep. Two are from Bordeaux, France. One looks like another case of brandy." Robert replied, "You should come up and we shall taste it. Maybe the French are trying to take the coast by other means."

The cottage was quiet. Catherine was at school. Mimmie and Rosie were not about. He sat at the dining room table and read his mail. There was a letter from the Admiralty.

You are hereby and forthwith etc. etc. by the First Lord of the Admiralty to report on or about August first this year of our Lord etc. etc. to attend a two-day conference of all Sea Fencible Commanders to present a plan of action for your designated area. Etc etc

The good Captain thought to himself, "Oh no the Admiralty again with London in high season. I am being punished." Davies came up to the cottage and they tested the brandy to be sure it was not poisoned. Davies had two glasses just to make sure. At least he would be home for the next two weeks to enjoy Catherine's company. When Catherine got home she was relieved to find that the letter was not a new sea-going command for her husband.

The village was quiet. Davies had hired Master Thornwell to work in the stable. Davies advised the good Captain that he had been replaced as the Friday stable hand. Robert, Tom, and John still enjoyed their Friday morning coffee and smoke together.

Robert went to his regular Tuesday business lunch at the Hancocks. He brought a bottle of the suspect French brandy to get the groups professional opinion on the safety of the brew. He told the group that he had to go to London on the first of August for meetings at the Admiralty. It was high season and rooms would be hard to find. Lord Eastman had an idea. "Robert as you know I have a townhome in London and have not visited in ages. Why don't I open it up and you and Catherine can be my guests!" Robert could see from his enthusiasm that the offer would be hard to refuse. Catherine had never been to London.

Robert said, "I thank you, my lord, that is a splendid idea." The wheels were in motion. Catherine would be very excited.

Lord Eastman wanted everything to be perfect. This was his first opportunity to spend time with the couple he admired most. The good Captain had a special place in his heart. He sent his butler James up to London a week ahead of time. He was to hire temporary staff. They needed an upstairs maid. A downstairs maid. A good cook was essential. He was to get tickets for the symphony, ballet, the opera if possible, and arrange to see some of London's special places. He also gave the assignment to find a female escort for Catherine who was familiar with London's fashion houses. Everything was in motion as the day approached.

Robert of course was traveling light with his sea chest. Catherine had her mother's wardrobe case, her father's bag and her own case. Sir Robert wondered if she was leaving for good.

Lambert and Abigail were happy about the trip for Catherine and were amazed and excited about their good friend John Eastmans enthusiasm for the trip.

They were off. Lord Eastman's coach picked them up. It took three days to get to London. Lord Eastman would not hear of Robert paying for anything. He was a splendid host.

His townhome was in an older fashionable part of London. It was not large but very impressive. James and the two maids met the coach as it arrived. Lord Eastman looked his property over. It was in splendid shape.

The couple was shown to their very large bed chamber and unpacked. James advised that dinner would be at 5:30. Catherine could not take her eyes off the large bathtub in the room. The upstairs maid sensing her ladyship's desire for a bath told her, "I will have a hot bath ready in a half-hour" and off she went.

Robert took a bottle of that fine suspect brandy and went downstairs to share it with Lord Eastman. He got a guided tour of the house. It was much bigger than Black Stone Cottage. The back garden was small. Most of the room was taken up by the coach house. Even James the butler was happy to be back in London. He could recall some very happy times here when Robert was a toddler and his mother accompanied Lord Eastman. James told Robert, "The happy times have returned."

This was Catherine's dream holiday. An afternoon bath followed by a wonderful dinner. She looked radiant. After dinner, a plan was devised. Robert would check in with the Admiralty a day early, but promised to be back in the early afternoon. Lord Eastman and Catherine would explore London's sites.

Next morning Robert was up at first light shaved, dressed, and downstairs. He startled the cook who did not expect any of the gentry to be up before nine. Robert explained as a naval Captain he was always up before the sun and only required biscuits and strong black coffee. He would be in the dining room arranging his papers. He was enjoying the house, but could not remember ever being here before.

While everyone slept Robert was off to the Admiralty. He arrived and went to the outer secretary. He was given a schedule for tomorrow. The Devon coast was eighth on the list. They would report promptly at the start of the Forenoon Watch. Captain Home Popham would preside over the meeting. Robert had never met him, but knew him by reputation. He was known as the intellectual Naval Captain who was developing a new signaling system for the Royal Navy. A good man to know.

Robert returned to the townhouse. Catherine and Lord Eastman had not returned from their tour of London. They hired a coachman for the whole week who was very familiar with London. The good Captain decided to spend the day fine-tuning his report. Mr Hicks had done a great job on the copies and maps. He was ready. He also sent a note to Lord Appleton to let him know that he and Lady Catherine were in town and would love to wait on him.

Catherine and his Lordship returned at two and advised that tonight it would be the symphony in the park. Catherine could not wait. It was another wonderful day.

Captain Sir Robert Burnes was at the Admiralty early the next morning. He signed in and went to the auditorium. Captain Home Popham was there. Robert introduced himself and was escorted to his seat. The meeting started precisely at the change of the watch. A number of Captains were late. Robert just shook his head. Captain Home Popham began with a quick overview. "Gentlemen, Napoleon continues to build a massive army across the channel. Regardless of the peace process, England's defense of the coast has become doubly important." There were three Admirals sitting in the back of the room. Most Captains were unprepared and just gave numbers. How many men. Numbers of equipment. Total hours trained etc. The Admirals were not kind to them. Some knew that they would be replaced and on half pay after this meeting was over.

Captain Popham introduced Captain Sir Robert Burnes of the Coast of Devon. Robert described the coast. He told them he got professional help from a retired Army Colonel to pick probable landing spots and why he discounted other areas. He then outlined the three locations and their role to defend each location. There was a detailed outline of his training program. Each Admiral had a copy of the plan. One of the Admirals asked how long he could stop a French attack? His response was, "Sir my Sea Fencibles can not stop them. We will only be able to slow them down until help arrives." It was going very well until he described his use of smugglers to gain intelligence on French activities on the Devon coast. This brought a lot of indignation from the audience.

"They should not be part of the Sea Fencibles command."

"Turn them into the Revenue Service."

"They should all be hanged."

Robert thought to himself "This is all going downhill. I should have quit while I was ahead." Then one of the Admirals rose in the back of the room and walked forward and spoke. "Gentlemen I have here a dispatch from the Port Admiral of Plymouth dated last month.

It has come to our attention by intelligence gained from the Sea Fencible Detachment at Exmouth that a French Corvette and Brig have been active on the Devon Coast and a date certain was given for their next operation. For three nights I dispatched a frigate and two Brigs to ambush them if they returned. On the night of 18 July, our forces intercepted the two French ships, sinking the Brig and badly damaging the Corvette before it escaped. The information obtained through local sources was instrumental in the success of this operation.

The Admiral looked to the group. "Gentlemen Bonaparte has a half million men ready to do England harm and we must use all sources at our disposal to defeat them. Well done, Captain Burnes. Thank you!" That ended any discussion and Robert beat a hasty retreat to his seat while he still had the weather gage. Robert was out the door at the end of the briefings before he was asked to down a pint or two with the other Captains.

Back at the townhouse, Cathrine had a wonderful day of shopping. The bed-chamber was filled with boxes. She was a happy lady. She announced that it was going to be an early supper and off to the ballet. Robert conceded it could not be worse than listening to all those presentations. Lord Eastman enjoyed watching the interplay between the two. They seemed to be of the same mind on almost everything and were most respectful of each other. What a fun couple to be with!

Robert was at the Admiralty early for the second day of the conference. He had no role to play. It was fun to watch some of the unprepared participants get a Royal Navy ass chewing. It was over before noon. Seven were asked to remain. Robert bet they were going to get their walking papers. Captain Home Popham had a brief discussion with him on the new signaling techniques and gave Sir Robert a copy of the new signal book which was being distributed to the fleet this year. Many of the officers at the Admiralty were discussing the possibilities of peace this year. It was time to get away from this puzzle palace and back to the real world.

Catherine and Lord Eastman had a fun day of shopping again. She found a precision telescope with a tripod for seeing very long distances. She also purchased a very well made foul weather jacket for Robert.

Robert arrived back at the residence first and decided that he would try the soaking bathtub. He was enjoying it when Catherine arrived back. As she entered the bed-chamber, she smiled, locked the door, unrobed, and joined him in the tub. It was a most enjoyable and amusing afternoon. They then dressed for dinner. Lord Eastman had invited some of his old friends to dinner. It was another very enjoyable evening. A messenger arrived with an invitation for the happy couple to join Lord Appleton for the Royal Opera. He would pick them up at three the next day. Lord Eastman's guests were impressed.

Catherine spent most of the next day in preparation for the evening. Robert had a relaxing morning talking to Lord Eastman about the state of affairs at home and the talk of peace. Robert enquired of Lord Eastman where he could get a soaking tub like the one upstairs. Catherine had completely enjoyed it.

THE ROYAL OPERA

Start of the First Dog Watch

Lord Appleton's coach arrived and he met Catherine for the first time and was delighted to make Lord Eastmans acquaintance. Lord Appleton gave Catherine his full attention. They were off to the Opera. All the carriages were arriving for the event. The footmen were opening doors to the carriages. Most of London's elite were checking each other out and trying to figure out who was the couple with the Duke of Farmington. (Lord Appleton) There was chamber music and a delightful buffet. Captain Home Popham caught Sir Robert's eye and was ushered off to have a polite conversation with the First Lord of the Admiralty. One of his junior Captains was here at the King's invitation. He wanted to determine where this officer was in the pecking order with the King. Lord Appleton the Duke and friend of the

King took Catherine under his protection and introduced her to all of London's upper crust. She felt like Cinderella at the ball.

Lord Appleton saw a nod from the King. He was being called to his presence. "Lady Catherine if you would join me, I shall introduce you to the King." The Royal entourage was standing with the King. The King spoke. "Appleton who is this pretty lady you have at your side?" The King was focused on the scar on her face which did not take away from her good looks. She was in that stunning gown and had that most exquisite stone at her breast. Appleton said, "Your Majesty May I present to you Lady Catherine Burnes, wife of Post Captain Sir Robert Burnes." Catherine bowed slowly and said, "Your Majesty." He replied, "Ah yes. Every Frenchman who sets to sea should fear two Englishmen in a rowboat. So this is the Lady behind the man. Welcome. Where is your husband?" She replied, "I am afraid he is in deep discussions with the First Lord, Your Majesty." The King wished her well. Told her to enjoy the Opera and reminded Lord Appleton that their card game for Tuesday was still on. With that the King moved on. Lady Charlotte watched from afar slightly amused.

Now the Lord Chamberlain with his assistants were getting everyone ready for the procession across the street to the Opera House. The Appleton party would be fifth in line. Robert joined them. "Sorry my

Darling, but duty calls. Did you have a good time?" Catherine put her hand through his arm. "I met the King."

The trumpets were now blaring. The street was roped off and the King's Guard was on full display. The crowd in the street was cheering.

In the foyer of the Opera House, they could hear the cheering. Viscount Torrington was explaining to his son and Lord Ransom with the two fluff head goddesses that he was not able to get an invitation to the King's reception. It was the toughest invite to get in London tonight. He had arranged with great expense to get them on the rope line here in the foyer. The ladies would be as close as fifty feet from the King. They both were excited. They would be able to tell their sister and parents that they were in the presents of the King.

The Lord Chamberlain came to the door and announced "His Majesty The King of England" and his followers. The fluff head goddesses bowed with reverence. Then the Prince of Wales and his followers were announced. The ladies were excited and thanked Lord Torrington with all their hearts. Then as the ladies looked on intently to get a good look at London's elite. The Lord Chamberlain announced, "The Duke of Farmington, Lord Appleton, and his guests Lady Catherine Burnes and Post Captain Sir Robert Burnes." The fluff head goddesses went bug-eyed. Their mouths could have dropped to the floor as they looked to each other. Catherine was walking erect head forward. She noticed her sisters. She smiled, gave them a nod, and proceeded on. The fluff head goddesses and their empty suit husbands could not believe what they had just seen. Catherine was in London! She was at the King's reception! Oh my God!

Viscount Torrington smiled. Burnes was a force to be reckoned with. The sooner his son figured this out the better off he would become. As they got to their orchestra seats, which were very good, they looked up to the box seats and there was Catherine sitting two boxes from the King. Catherine saw her sisters and waved. It was a night to remember.

During the intermission, Robert went to get some refreshments. Lady Charlotte who was in the box with the Prince of Wales made her move. She appeared at the door to the box larger than life and completely overdressed. She nodded to Lord Appleton and looked to Catherine. "So you are Robert's wife. I am Lady Charlotte. Your husband saved my life a number of years back."

"An honor to meet you." was Catherine's response. "Robert has gone to get some refreshments." She could sense this woman was very overbearing and trouble. Lady Charlotte said, "I have not seen you on London's social scene." Catherine, wanting to get away from this woman replied, "No, with Robert at sea much of the time we are busy at home."

Robert walked through the door holding two glasses of Champagne. Before Catherine could say anything Lady Charlotte said, "There is my lord protector. You look well. It is good to see you again.

Oh dear, the Second Act is about to begin. The Prince will wonder what has happened to me." She smiled at Robert and was gone. Catherine gloved hands to her face and was laughing. "Oh, Robert you know that woman?" Sir Robert responded, "I rescued her from highwaymen before my time in Riverton." Catherine with a chuckle said, "I bet you did. Good God! I would not trust that woman in a stable yard with a billy goat." They both started laughing.

"Indeed my love. A billy goat?"

"Yes, in fact she could seduce a priest in a confessional. Oh, Robert." as she started to chuckle again. Lord Appleton intervened." I am glad you two are having such a wonderful time. It makes my heart glad." Cathrine said, "It will be a night I long remember." As she hugged her husband, and it was. She never brought up Lady Charlotte again.

Lord Appleton's coach dropped them off at Lord Eastman's townhome. He bid them farewell. Robert thanked him profusely and said, "Goodnight." Lord Appleton said, "God bless you both. You are fine people."

The next morning Catherine and Robert's bags were loaded on the back of the coach. To Robert's surprise, the bathtub was tied to the top of the coach.

Lord Eastman said, "It is a gift from me. It will get no use sittings upstairs and I know Catherine will enjoy it." The trip home was wonderful. Lord Eastman was really enjoying the time with Catherine and Robert. They had a wonderful time. A better time for John Eastman had not been had in many years.

PEACE HAS COME

Middle Watch

The summer was coming to a close. The fluff head goddesses were less than two months from providing their husbands with heirs to the estates. The crops from the valley were in full harvest. Catherine still lived in the afterglow of her trip. She felt wonderful. The Sea Fencibles were now organized and Lieutenant Maxfield was married.

Captain Burnes was enjoying life at home again and was still on full pay. Then in September, the news came. The war with France was over. It was called the Peace of Amiens. It did not feel like peace. No battle has decided the outcome. It was more like a breather. They had been at war for nine years. In Riverton, it would be known as the quiet time.

The village was very quiet. Sir Robert, John Hicks, and Tom Davies enjoyed their Friday mornings with coffee and smokes. Every Friday night the boys joined the locals at the Tally Ho for a wet. Abigail, Mimmie, and Catherine continued their practice three times a week. Lambert Hancock had his business fine-tuned to the harvest season. There was money to be made.

England was at war with no one at the moment. When everything is working smoothly, get ready for the unexpected.

THE VILLAGE RESPONDS

Two Bells in the Afternoon Watch

It was a quiet, pleasant Friday in Riverton. Everyone was out and about. It was market day. Lady Catherine and Rosie were passing by the stable. Joshua Thornwell was cleaning out the stable and bid them a good afternoon. Davies gave them a wave from the smithy. Mr. Hicks was headed into the Tally Ho. Catherine's first stop was the butcher shop. As she crossed the street she noticed that everyone was looking back up the street towards Mountain Road. There was Skully's young wife Amie staggering down the middle of the street. Someone was shouting to get the Millets, Amies parents. Catherine moved quickly up the street. She was shocked. "My dear God! What has happened to you my child?" She was a child of fourteen or fifteen. Her face was beaten to a pulp. One eye was swollen shut. She was holding her baby.

The girl was in shock. Catherine was holding her until her family arrived. She asked, "What happened?" Her only answer was, "He beat me again." Catherine could not believe it. "Your husband Mr. Skully who lives on our property did this!" By now thirty or so people were in the street. Catherine instructed Rosie, "Go get Captain Burnes. It is urgent."

As Rosie ran past the smithy Davies knew there was a problem. He told young Thornwell to get Mr. Hicks. As Rosie explained to Sir Robert, he instinctively put on his pocket pistol, his work jacket, and was out the door. Tom and John joined him at the smithy. "Gentlemen something is amiss. Please follow me." Members of the crowd watched as Sir Robert arrived. They commented, "Finally something will be done. Skully has abused that poor girl for far too long.

Our Lord and Lady will put a stop to it." Robert looked at the poor girl. Catherine was holding Amie and the baby upright. Robert furiously said, "Dear God! Skully did this to you?" It was beat to quarters time for the good Captain. "Mr Hicks get your writing satchel and then go find the Magistrate. Mr. Davies I believe some tools of our trade are required."

Robert marched up the street with everyone following. The crowd grew as they got to the road behind the Tally Ho. Davies came out of the smithy armed to the teeth and instructed Thornwell, "Come with me." The Magistrate arrived and everyone in the

Tally Ho knew that something big was up. They followed the crowd. The Millets arrived to comfort their daughter. The Thornwells also joined watching their son with Mr Davies. As they got to the gate of Robert and Catherine's 50-hectare property Robert stopped everyone at the gate. Amie looked to the Captain. "He is drunk." Robert asked, "Does he have a gun?"

"Yes My Lord, he has a fowling-piece his father gave to him." Robert gave the orders. "Mr. Hicks back of the building if you please. Mr. Davies, we shall be at the front door." The crowd knew the Captain meant business. He had his pistol out. They went to the front door. Davies looked in the window. The scoundrel was drunk and sitting at a table. Robert said, "Ready" and they went through the front door. As everyone watched a shot rang out. Catherine was holding her breath. There was quite a commotion coming from the cottage. After a few minutes, Robert came outside and waved to Catherine.

Hicks and Davies were dragging Skully out to the gate in front of the crowd. Almost all of the village was there by then. Skully was bleeding profusely from the head and nose. Robert began the interrogation. "Did you do this to your wife and child?"

Skully said, "Of course I did. What's it to you? She is my property and I can do as I wish."

"Mr. Davies," said with a nod by Robert and Skully got an elbow to the ribs. It hurt. Robert decided to take another tact. "Assault on a defenseless woman is a criminal offense. Skully in his alcoholic stupor said, "Who the hell cares about that little piece of crap." Robert answered, "I do Sir. Mr. Davies!" He hit him with another blow. This one took him to his knees. The villagers seemed to feel that justice was being served to this despicable man. "What shall we do with you Mr. Skully? You attack a defenseless woman of our village?" Robert asked. Skully, still drunk said, "I don't give a damn. The little wench is mine." He laughed. Robert said, "Mr. Davies" who now slammed him in the head. He fell to the ground. They picked him up. Robert told him "You are a slow learner sir." Skully realized that maybe he had had enough. "What do you want from me?" Robert looked to the Millets and their daughter. Then to the Thornwells and their son who had clenched fists and was crying for his school sweetheart. Robert smiled at Catherine.

He had an idea.

"Magistrate, is there still a custom in old English law to sell your wife at the stump and is binding on the purchaser to take the lady as his wife?" The Magistrate looked to Robert, "Yes, I believe the contract would be binding." Catherine had no idea what Robert was doing. Robert said, "Very well then Skully do you agree to sell the lady at the stump?" Skully smiled. "What the hell. I don't care."

"Very well, the Magistrate would you conduct the sale." The Magistrate turned to the crowd. "What am I bid for this lady and her child?" Two of Skully's blokes in the crowd nodded to him and said, "Two shillings with a laugh. Amie's parents were quite concerned as was Catherine. Robert had it all under control as he said, "I bid £5 in the name of Mister Joshua Thornwell." The crowd was amazed. The Magistrate asked, "Are there any other bids? Very well. The bidding is concluded. SOLD." Robert asked Mr Hicks to write a formal bill of sale transferring the property of Mr. Skully to Master Thornwell. In a few minutes, they signed and Robert paid the £5. He handed the paper to Joshua, shook his hand, and said, "Congratulations. You are a married man." He then looked to Catherine who was holding the young lady with her parents. "I hope your life now will be much improved." Mrs. Millet was crying and said, "God bless you, Sir. You have saved my daughter from a living hell." Robert was not finished. "If the Thornwells and Millets will remain Catherine and I wish to speak to you."

He went back to Skully and told him, "You have five minutes to get off my property. If you two gentlemen will conduct him to the cottage and let him get his personal effects, clothes and the like and then escort him out of town on South Road." Robert let him know "If you return to the village of Riverton ever again there will be hell to pay from everyone in the village." Mr Davies and Mr Hicks followed by twenty of the townspeople escorted him out of town.

Catherine took Amie and her baby to the cottage with Mrs. Millet and Mrs Thornwell. Robert presented his plan to father and son. "I need a new tenant for this property. I see not much of it can be planted but the hillside is good grazing land. Mr. Thornwell, I understand you are familiar with sheep. He answered, "I am My Lord." Robert looked to young Thornwell. "You now have a family to support. We did not start out on the best of terms, but Mr. Davies tells me you are a good worker. If you are interested I need a new tenant on this holding. I would expect the rent to be paid on time and that it turns a profit within two years. Are you up to the challenge?" Joshua answered, "I am Sir. Thank you." They shook hands. "Mr. Hicks will be along with some papers for you to sign." He looked to his father. "Is it Suffolk or Dorset Mr. Thornwell?" He was surprised by Robert's knowledge. "Well Sir, Dorset brings higher prices at the mill, but Soffolk are better breeding." Robert said, "I will leave it to the experts. When you have a plan, bring it to Black Stone Cottage and I will fund it."

"Thank you, Sir Robert. We are very grateful."

Catherine joined him and they bid the family good day and headed down the lane. Robert looked to his bride, "Well my love are you happy with the outcome?"

"My goodness husband you are quick to act. Ever the Captain." She said as she smiled and laughed.

They walked home arm in arm with the whole village watching and giving a silent thank you.

Davies was back at the smithy and Molly was scolding him. "You have blood on that shirt."

Davies replied, "Ain't mine so don't you worry none."

Lord and Lady returned to Blackstone Cottage. No groceries were purchased today. They would live on love tonight.

IT WAS TIME

Morning Watch

At the end of autumn, nature told the two fluff head goddesses that the time had come. Elizabeth and her husband at his father's request were headed to Great Torrington to Viscount Torrington's estate to give birth. At least Victoria would give birth in Riverton at the Ransom Estate. Lord and Lady Ransom the father and mother of Victoria's husband kept to their estate most of the time and never participated in the social events of the valley. They left that to young Sir Kenneth and Victoria.

Lady Ransom was very much in charge at the birth and left Abigail and Lambert as spectators in the blessed event. On the day of the happenings Lambert, Abigail, Mimmie, and Lady Catherine were left in the foyer while everything happened upstairs. This hurt Abigail deeply, but she said nothing. Their son in law came downstairs to advise it was a girl. He and his father were not very happy. At the correct time, the Hancocks got invited upstairs to congratulate their daughter and hold their grandchild. There was no celebration or toasts. It just happened. The family went home.

Then two days later they got word that Elizabeth gave birth to a girl on the same day as her sister. This brought a chuckle from the whole family. The twins seemed to do everything together including birth. The Hancocks felt left out. Their daughters were members of the peerage class. They were just rich commoners. Catherine tried to console them. She promised that things would be different when her time came.

Lambert knew that the tension would mount with his sons in law until both daughters produced heirs. This was not working like he had planned when they got married. He still had Robert and Catherine and he could not be happier about that. He was enjoying his time with Robert. He had a good head on his shoulders. Lambert would have to count his blessing that one out of three is not bad. He and John Eastman were great friends and the old Colonel added great humor to the threesome. Life has a plan. Lambert just wished that God would let him in on it.

THE CHAMBER POT

Four Bells in the Afternoon Watch

The end of the war left the good Captain with a lot of time on his hands and a routine in the Navy that called for 16-18 hour days. He had a logical mind that needed to be engaged. He needed to find a problem and put his energy to work solving it.

Catherine and Robert put the soaking tub in the closet under the roof at the top of the stairs. It was an eight by ten-foot room with a sloping roof and a dormer window for light. One wall was next to the chimney so the room stayed warm in winter.

Robert resolved to solve a problem that had haunted England since ancient times. What to do with human waste in the household. The chamber pot had been in existence for centuries. The whole system of defecation removal seemed archaic. He had grown up on board a ship where this was not a problem. There was no smell, storage, or removal issues. You sat on the seat of ease. You expunged substance. Poured a bucket of seawater down the hole and it was washed out the lubber hole and into the sea. At home, this was a particular problem for the ladies and outside facilities were not the answer.

Robert explained his idea to Mr Hicks and Mr Davies. The boys at the smithy had a good laugh about it over coffee on Friday morning. Davies said, "So we are working on a new system of cack removal." Mr. Hicks chinned in, "Since the Irish invented the stuff I believe it is called cac. Short for caca." Davies responded, "English merchantmen call it S.H.I.T. for Stow High In Transit. If it gets wet it gives off a gas that explodes in the bilge when near a candle." Mr. Hicks, not to be outdone "The Germans call it kacken." Robert decided that there was no support here. He decided to bring the discussion back to the problem. "We need a system as we have onboard ship. Any ideas gentlemen?" Hicks and Davies were beginning to think that war must be declared again because they were losing the Captain.

Robert would not let it go. There must be a solution. His mission was to eliminate the chamber pot without human hands touching the foul substance. It would be a wonderful gift for the ladies. But how?

In a week he had an idea and it involved the tub closet at the top of the stairs and Sir Issac Newton's theories put to practical use.

Robert brought it up at his regular Tuesday meeting at the Hancocks. They had a bigger laugh than the boys at the smithy. Robert let it go. He was going to solve this waste removal problem.

At dinner he let it be known to the ladies that he was working on a solution to the chamber pot. Catherine without looking up from her dinner said, "Oh really." She and Mimmie started to laugh hysterically. He could even hear Rosie laughing in the kitchen. There was no respect for his idea in this house.

He concluded that everyone wanted to talk about caca, but no one wanted to deal with it.

Robert was not deterred. He sat at the table with lead and paper drawing up ideas. He went to the Hancocks brick making operation to discuss the clay pipe he needed. He also asked about a large bowl to replace the chamber pot. He was advised there was such a maker in Exeter.

Winter was coming. He needed to act on his idea now. Robert allocated £100 to the project. Davies got him four good men with strong backs to dig the hole. He picked the back of the cottage that sloped slightly from the house. The workers dug an eight-foot diameter hole five feet deep and five trenches extending from the hole, a foot deep like fingers sloping down. They were twenty feet long. They then dug a trench from the hole to the base of the house under the closet area. Sir Robert put the brick masons to work bricking the whole thing in and a chimney lined in the pipe all the way up the side of the house with a hole entering the closet and a regular chimney cap on top. He ran a clay pipe from the base of the chimney to the eight-foot hole or receptacle as he called it. The ladies had no idea what was going on but showed Abigail anyway. No one asked any questions. They were afraid of what the answer might be. No chamber pot! What is the world coming to?

The circular hole and the trenches were lined in brick. The trenches were covered in slate and Robert hired a carpenter to cover the pit in oak planking. Then he and Davies covered the oak in sailcloth and tarred the whole thing over. They spread dirt over the whole area and seeded it for the spring growth.

No one asked any questions. They were not sure of the folly of this enterprise, but the good Captain gave it his full attention.

He and Catherine used Lord Eastman's coach to go to Exeter to pick up his oversized chamber pot with a five-inch flared hole in the bottom. It curved outward at the top and was funneled to the whole in the bottom. It was the craziest request they have ever made. They made a cover for it, even as none had been requested. They were all puzzled by it. Catherine returned with packages from shopping. Robert came back with the most unbelievable chamber pot known to mankind.

The mason took up the floorboards in the closet and cemented in the pipe which curved upward flush with the new oak floor. He had the walls plastered and a special seat made at Lambert's wood manufacture.

It was done. Robert tested it when everyone was gone. On Saturday he invited everyone to the cottage for the unveiling. No one was sure how to respond to the good Captain. He took it all in stride. They had a toast in the parlor then marched everyone upstairs for the demonstration.

The ladies were most amused. The men were ready, willing, and able to test the new idea. One by one they took their turn and deposited their load so to speak. After the bucket was dumped and the deposit disappeared down the lubber hole just like in the ship. Everyone including the ladies inspected the pot and confirmed it was empty.

Back in the parlor, Robert explained in detail the workings of the system. Everyone pretended to understand. Robert announced that his cottage now had a water closet for the convenience of the ladies. For the next week, everyone was checking in with Catherine to see if it was working and had the Captain returned to his good senses?

After a few weeks, Catherine noticed a smell coming from the hole. Robert determined that not all the gasses were going up the chimney. He devised a wood stopper wrapped in leather to be placed in the hole after each use. He had a small rope attached to pull it out.

Water was poured over the top to ensure the seal. The ladies reported no more smell. They were taking more baths now and Mimmie painted flowers on the pot.

Davies was declaring to the world. "Bloody Hell, but the Captain's invention works, and that ain't no error!" Word spread that a Navy Sea Captain from the village of Riverton in Devon had solved one of England's most pressing problems. The Chamber Pot!

THE INVENTOR

Start of the First Dog Watch

It was Friday night again. Everyone at the Tally Ho was talking about the Captain's invention. The Magistrate and uncle George decided that Robert should apply for status on his idea by filing with the Kings commissioner of patents and inventions. The Magistrate looked up the laws. Robert and Mr. Hicks provided the description and diagrams of the whole system. They called it "A system of waste disposal." It sounded very impressive. Tom Davies called it like it was. "Caca flows downhill." They had all the required documentation including a £120 fee. The group laughed as Robert told them, "It is more than I spent building it." They sent it off by the post rider. Davies said, "Well sir, you can kiss that money goodbye." Robert had no complaints. The system continued to work and the ladies were happy. In fact, everyone wanted to try it out.

A few weeks went by and Robert was with Lambert at their Tuesday luncheon when Catherine came in barring a letter from the Court of Saint James. He had been awarded approval from the King for his invention. The King's seal was on the document. No one in the group was laughing anymore. Captain Sir Robert Burnes was now an inventor of record. Lambert and Lord Eastman were asking if one could be installed in their residences? Robert would look into it after he got back from Exmouth. He had to help Lieutenant Maxfield. Now that the war was over he was having a hard time keeping the Sea Fencible Command together. No one feared the press gangs any longer. He would be back in a week.

Davies was at the smithy when the latest coach arrived and a man dressed in a black business suit got out and was inquiring about the residence of Robert Burnes. Davies did not like the look of the man as he went into the Tally Ho. A short time later he was headed up the path to Black Stone Cottage.

Catherine answered the door. The man was not polite. He demanded, "I must speak to Robert Burnes NOW. I have a rite to serve him. Where is he?" Catherine tried to explain, "He is with his Sea Fencibles in Exmouth." The man would not leave and was very disrespectful. Mimmie came downstairs. Catherine told Rosie, "Go get Mr. Davies quick."

When Davies got to the door Catherine was crying. No more needed to be said. Davies had the man by the scruff of the neck and the back of his pants. The man in black was screaming, "I am an officer of the court. How dare you!" Davies was having none of it. No one makes Lady Catherine cry. It just so happened that the two o'clock coach was ready to depart. Davies manhandled him into the coach and told the driver, "Hank! I want this here villain out of the village now." The driver replied, "Sure Tom, anything you say." And off they went. Tom and Molly went up to the cottage to check on Catherine. She was alright but had no idea what the creepy man wanted. He left no papers.

Tom assured the ladies. "That is the last time they would see him."

Robert got home and everyone was confused by the incident. On Friday morning at the smithy, Robert thanked Tom for his quick action. Everyone thought that would be the end of it all. It wasn't.

The next Wednesday a coach arrived and the same man and three others got off the coach. They got rooms at the inn and asked to speak to the local Magistrate. Mr. Hicks told them he would fetch him. He alerted Tom who went right up to the cottage. Rosie was sent to get Mr. Hancock. Robert put his pocket pistol on and he and Davies headed for the Tally Ho. No scoundrel would ever scare Lady Catherine again. They met Lambert, Mr. Hicks, and the Magistrate at the door. Robert looked to the group. "Gentlemen!

Let's be about our business." The group of four, with three dressed in black business suits and one was well dressed in a gentleman's business attire. Robert approached the group. Everyone in the Tally Ho expected trouble. Robert said, "I am Captain Sir Robert Burnes. I understand that you gentlemen are looking for me." Robert looked to Davies, "Which one is he, Tom?" Davies pointed to the older man. Robert stared him down. "Out or I will throw you out of my uncle's establishment." The younger man said, "There must be some misunderstanding." Robert cut him off. "He treated my wife deplorably and I demand satisfaction." Davies looked to his Captain and thought, "Mother of God. The Captain is calling him out and I forgot my pistol." The four visitors did not know it yet, but they were outnumbered by twentyfold in the Tally Ho. The younger man in black sensed that they were in trouble and said to his partner. "He's a Post Captain in the Royal Navy. How did we miss that Mr. Spittal?" Trying to intimidate this crowd would not end well. "Forgive me, Captain Burnes, I am Mr. Shadbolt and this is my partner Mr. Spittal. Our firm represents the interests of the Cummings who hold the original patent on the indoor receptacle approved by the King in 1775." Robert was surprised that this idea goes back some 28 years. Robert asked, "What does this have to do with me?" The arrogant Mr. Spittal jumped in. "You must cease and desist from using this design. We are tired of dealing with every country bumpkin with a title before their name." Robert, ever the Captain said," Mr. Davies, Mr. Hicks kindly escort this despicable person from my uncle's establishment. In fact Sir, you owe Lady Catherine a sincere apology for your conduct in my home." With that, the boys grabbed him by the arms and unceremoniously deposited him on the bench outside the Tally Ho.

The man in the eloquent business attire spoke. "Forgive us, Sir Robert, I am John Crapper and I am responsible for putting the design in large production. Would you like to see the production design?"

Meanwhile, Molly had summoned the ladies to the Tally Ho. They all appeared as a group Catherine, Mimmie, and Abigail. Catherine looked the despicable man in the eye. Davies made him stand up. "Now bow to Lady Catherine and make your apology." Spittal did this with great reluctance. Catherine curtsied to him and said, "Good day Sir. Is Sir Robert in the Tally Ho Tom?" Tom nodded yes. Catherine said, "Let's see what my husband is about." Davies pushed the man back into his seat. "You ain't going nowhere May-tee."

The ladies sat at a table in the back of the dining room to watch the proceedings. Robert was looking at the 1775 patent. His comment was, "This is quite an elegant design." Mr. Crapper commented, "All of the piping is glazed like china so there is no sticking to the surface." Robert asked, "What is the S-shaped pipe for?" Crapper with pride said, "The water in the trap prevents gasses from coming back up the pipe."

"Ah yes. I see the benefit of it and it is much simpler than my stopper mechanism." Robert thought to himself, "This design makes mine look amateurish." The Magistrate asked, "If the patent approval was in 1775 then it would have been an open public design by 1800." Mr. Shadbolt was ready for this question. "This patent was approved before the change in law and we believe is still in force."

Robert was puzzled. "How does this affect me? I have a valid patent with the King's seal." Shadbolt replied, "The war is over and we wish to get into full production without a legal battle on our hands. We are prepared to reimburse you the cost of your patent and offer another £100 for your inconvenience." Robert answered, "I am quite confused. If you say that my design is inferior. I would agree, but it is functional and would cost less to implement." The man who never introduced himself looked to the barrister and nodded. Shadbolt said, "In good faith, we would extend the offer to £200." Robert asked Mr. Hancock to join him with the ladies to see if they needed any refreshments.

Robert asked Catherine, "Was the apology acceptable?" She answered, "It was and Tom made him bow to me." as she chuckled. Robert asked Lambert with all the ladies listening intently, "What do you make of this? Why do they want my patent? Their design is far superior. I have no idea who the third man is but he is obviously the money behind the venture. There has to be something else." Father Lambert could offer no good explanation. Robert's mind was working over-time. They rejoined the group.

Robert took the lead and said, "Gentlemen I thank you for your kind offer, but I see that my design will be much cheaper. I concede that it will be a little less convenient. I do not see it as competition for your design." The money man nodded to Shadbolt who said, "We are prepared to make a final offer of £400."

Lambert did not know what to make of it. That offer got the ladies' attention. Robert asked to look at Crapper's design again. The men in black seemed to be very irritated. As he looked at the design it dawned on him. "This design is about eliminating the chamber pot itself. My patent is about a system that would include the seat of ease but was so much more in that it dealt with the waste and how to dispose of it after it left the house."

Robert thought to himself. "I believe I have the weather gage on them. Now let's give them a broadside and see what they do." Catherine commented to Abigail, "It appears that my wonderful husband has things well in hand." Robert looked to the man in black that never identified himself. "Sir, I believe you represent Cummings' interest in this enterprise. I do recognize your most thoughtful design. I also recognize the value of my system that will have the effect of law for the next seventeen years on your design. I, therefore, would like you to consider my proposal. If you wish to obtain the rights to my design I shall require £2,000 and maintain the rights to execute my system wherever I choose. As part of the bargain Mr. Crapper, you will provide me thirty of your design including piping and S pipes at no cost." Things went very quiet. Lambert almost fell off his chair. He decided that he would never play cards against Robert. Sir Robert looked to his lady and smiled. She flirted with him by winking back at him. Shadbolt went on a five-minute temper tantrum. The man in black and Mr Crapper remained quiet. Crapper nodded to the man in black. Robert thought to himself, "I have won." The man in black said, "You are a shrewd negotiator Sir Robert. We have underestimated you. We agree to your three terms." The ladies shouted with glee. Lambert patted Robert on the back. Everyone in the Tally Ho knew that their hometown hero had won again.

Mr. Shadbolt said, "I will send documents for your signature." Robert answered, "The Magistrate and Mr. Hicks can draw up documents within the hour. Mr. Hicks, would you join us, please? Your services are needed." Shadbolt said, "This is most irregular Sir." Robert smiled at him and said, "This is how we small-town bumpkins with a title before our name do it."

The ladies retired and Abigail advised, "Dinner would be at four at the house to celebrate the day. All would be welcome. Molly went outside to check on Tom. Molly hands on her hips said, "Thomas please let that poor man go." Davies told him, "I hope you have learned your lesson for the Captain was prepared to end your miserable life." Davies obeyed Molly's order.

Within the hour documents were signed. The three men in black could not wait to get out of this backwater town. Mr. Crapper had a parting comment to Sir Robert. "Our water closet design will revolutionize the world and my name will go down in history," Robert shook his hand and said, "I believe it will Mr. JOHN CRAPPER!"

THE WINTER OF PEACE

Morning Watch

Life that winter was centered around Black Stone Cottage. There were quiet evenings in the parlor in front of the fire. Rosie would make wonderful dinners for the family and guests. They all still marveled at the water closet. Robert was working on a design and construction for the Hancocks and Lord Eastman. There was very little correspondence from the Admiralty. It was as if the rest of the world had forgotten them. The smithy was still very busy and Robert got his job back cleaning the stable on Fridays. Both of his lease holdings started to prosper. He now had sheep grazing on the hillside. Robert asked Davies to be the overseer for the tenants. They found it easier to talk to Tom than his Lordship.

Catherine's sisters and their husbands were still as arrogant as ever but would be less rich this coming year. With peace, the sea lanes were open from the Low Countries and Germany. Grain production flowed to England. Prices would be much lower next year. Invitations never came so the only time they had to put up with them was at the Hancocks parties and dinners. Mr. Hicks was still a fixture around the cottage. Molly would stop by occasionally for tea. They would have Sunday breakfast with Robert's aunt and uncle before church. The ladies would practice on Sunday afternoon. Catherine was loving all the attention she was getting from Robert. For his birthday she got him a gentle little mare called Smokey. Lord Eastman provided the saddle and harness. Davies said it was a yeoman horse. It did whatever the Captain told it to do.

The winter turned to spring. Life was quiet and happy. It could go on forever. They all got lulled into a false sense of security.

THE LIEUTENANT

Two bells in the forenoon watch

Every Friday Robert would spend the day working with Davies at the Smithy. He was wearing ships slops work clothes and after coffee left Davies and Hicks to go clean the stable. As he was taking the old hay out, a horseman appeared at the stable door. "You there! Would you take care of my mount? Please feed and water him." Robert responded, "Yes Sir. Would you like the horse stabled?" Robert had a big smile on his face as the horseman was in full naval uniform with the rank of Lieutenant. He asked, "What will you charge?" Robert pointed to Davies. "You will have to ask the owner." He dismounted, grabbed his satchel, and asked Davies, "I am looking for Captain Sir Robert Burnes. I have an urgent dispatch for him from the Admiral at Plymouth." Both Davies and Hicks had big smiles on their faces. Davies said, "I believe I can direct you to him, Sir." The Lieutenant looked at him impatiently. "Well!" Robert looked to the group. "Mr. Hicks would you kindly get the dispatch from the Lieutenant."

"Aye Sir" The young Lieutenant looked at the stable hand with a horrified expression on his face. "Sir I beg your pardon but." Robert cut him off. "Mr. Hicks would you kindly get the young gentleman a room at my uncle's inn. Advise him that dinner is at two bells in the first watch at the cottage. I must get this horse rubbed down and fed."

"Forgive me Sir I did not realize." Robert cut him off again."Don't be late and Mr. Hicks if he has his journal with him, please bring that to the cottage as well."

Davies took the horse from the Captain laughing loudly. Mr. Hick told the Lieutenant to follow him. He had a big grin on his face. The young officer just felt like he had stepped in horse dung big time.

Robert went to the cottage and advised Catherine that they would have a guest for dinner, a young naval lieutenant. Mr. Hicks arrived with the dispatch and journal. "Sir the young man is beside himself. His name is Grayson and is the nephew of the Port Admiral."

"Splendid we shall lay on the dog for him at dinner and our best Port. I am sure Rosie can whip something up for us on short notice." Catherine and Mimmie were now in full preparation mode. Waste not a minute.

At precisely two bells in the first dog watch (5 PM) there was a knock at the door. Mr. Hicks answered. "Good evening Lieutenant. The Captain and the ladies are in the parlor." The Lieutenant walked in and stood to attention. "Forgive me Sir for my indiscretion this afternoon."

Robert said, "Yes, well Lieutenant we should always be prepared for the unexpected in the Navy.

Lieutenant Grayson may I present Lady Catherine and her Aunt Mimmie. Mr. Hicks would you open the wine for us. Please sit down." Grayson was a little intimidated by the Captain's humble home but saw that everyone was very comfortable in their surroundings. He also noticed the large scar on the Captain's right cheek and Lady Catherine's scar on her left cheek. They were still a very handsome couple. It was a very relaxing meal. Rosie was at her best when under pressure. Mr. Hicks poured the port after dinner and Robert gave him a glass. The young Lieutenant drank to the King and then expected the ladies to retire. They did not. Robert led the conversation." I read the letter from Admiral Grayson. Please let him know I am at his disposal. I will leave for Plymouth the day after tomorrow. Now without letting the cat out of the bag, please let us in on what is going on." Grayson looked to the ladies. Robert smiled." I have no secrets from Lady Catherine so please continue."

"Well Sir the Admiralty paid Admiral Grayson a visit and wanted to know how many ships he could put to sea on short notice. Four ships have Captains who are in London at the moment. I believe my uncle will appoint jobbing (temporary) Captains if the need arrives. He has a number of sealed orders which can only be opened on signal from London." Robert's reply was, "So it begins again! I am surprised the peace lasted this long with Boney still building a massive army across the channel ready to pounce on England." Catherine and Mimmie were surprised to be let in on such confidential information. "Please tell the Admiral I am grateful for his confidence. Here is your journal. You can tell a lot about an officer from his writing. You are a very detailed and accurate officer. Mr. Hicks will escort you to the inn. I am sure you would like to get an early start in the morning." He thanked the ladies for the hospitality and bid them a good evening.

Robert had already given instructions that Hicks and Davies were to provide hospitality at the bar in the Tally Ho and that Lieutenant Grayson was to leave with the biggest hangover of his life.

Next morning John Hicks started packing the Captain's sea chest. Robert had a confidential conversation with Lambert and Abigail and bid them farewell. Robert had been home over two years and Catherine felt lonely even before his departure. That night, in the bed-chamber, as they opened the bonds between them, Catherine let him know her secret. She was with child and about two months along. Robert was excited beyond belief. "My love I will be back to you as soon as possible. These Jobbing Captain assignments don't last long. The permanent Captain always finds a way to get to his ship." They held each other until sleep found them.

THE NEW COMMAND

Two Bells in the afternoon Watch

It was May and everything was in bloom. They arrived in Plymouth on the afternoon coach. John Hicks took the baggage and went to the inn to see about rooms. There were at least ten ships in the harbor. It was not the bustle of activity he expected. It was still the sleepy peacetime seaport it had been the last eighteen months. However, the Port Admirals office was a buzz of activity. Robert checked in with the admiral's secretary. "I am sorry Sir but Admiral Grayson has a meeting with the victualing yard, the armory, and the chandlers office. We are short of everything at the moment. I will let him know you have arrived. I will get word to you at the inn when things settle down."

Robert went to the inn and found that Mr. Hicks had gotten them the last room available. There were a number of officers in the lobby, but he did not recognize any of them. All ships officers were asked to return to their ships. They were saying their goodbyes to wives and lovers. Robert and Mr. Hicks retired to the main room and enjoyed an ale. Robert watched and said, "It appears this establishment will be clearing out very quickly."

In the late afternoon, a midshipman appeared looking for Captain Burnes. "Forgive me Sir, but Admiral has asked me to fetch you." The Port Admirals office was quiet now. Robert reported to Admiral Grayson "Good afternoon Sir. It appears you have your hands full at the moment."

"Aye, Sir Robert. That would be an understatement. No ship in this port has a full complement of officers and crew. They are all low on victuals, powder, and some need work at the yard before going to sea. Robert asked, "How can I be of assistance." The Admiral looked out the window at the harbor. "I have a mission for you and a twenty-four gun frigate that is in need of a Captain. The Captain just sent me a letter to hold his ship for him. He would be down in two or three weeks. The arrogance of the man to tell an Admiral to hold his ship!" Grayson was agitated. "He is a member of parliament, but in the King's Navy, he is but a Post Captain. I am going to give you command of *HMS Peacock*. I am going to send you on a long journey so plan at least six months. The ship is undermanned. It is low on ships stores. The Captain took his full entourage with him to London. His clerk, servant, coxswain, and his followers. His nephew just returned and is back on board. He brought word from his uncle to hold his ship. Blackwell is a very arrogant egotistical man." Robert's ears perked up. "Did you say Blackwell Sir?"

"Do you know him?"

"Aye Sir. I served under him in the *Hermione* when I was a midshipman." Robert thought "Well this is poetic justice." Robert asked, "What do I need to do?" Grayson with a frown on his face said, "You are low on the list to get serviced I am afraid. You will have to fend for yourself. Perhaps if a few palms are greased you may get the provisions you need. I will have orders for you tomorrow. I am sorry we will not be able to dine together." As Robert was leaving the Admiral said, "By the way William Denholm is at the East India Company office if you would like to pay your respects."

"Thank you, Sir, I will be delighted to see him."

Mr. Hicks was waiting for him outside. "Come Mr. Hicks. Waste not a minute." They went to the victualing yard. It was turmoil. They did not have any request from the *Peacock*. They then stopped to see if there had been a request for powder. There was none available. It would appear that the ship's Captains who were here had seen that their ships got first shot at all supplies. Robert told Mr Hicks to return to the inn. He was going to visit the Director of the East India Company.

He went to the John Company office and asked for Mr. William Denholm. The good Captain was in luck. He was in. "Sir Robert it is good to see you again." Mr. Denholm introduced his associates to the Captain. "It has been four years or so since you interrupted the French scheme in the islands and saved the company considerable sums of money." Robert said, "I thank you, Sir. The days on the *Seahawk* were very good indeed. Now it would appear we are to stop the French again. I have a ship at anchor short of everything and it would appear we are late to the party. In this port the cupboards are bare." Mr. Denholm asked, "What ship have they given you?"

"The *Peacock* Sir, as a jobbing Captain." Mr. Denholm shook his head. "It is our good friend of the common man in Parliament Mr. Blackwell. Well, at least he will be stuck on land for a while. Watch yourself, Sir Robert. He is not to be trusted."

"Aye Sir, I have served with him before and he has left his mark on my life. Thank you for the advice, but my concern now is to provide victuals, stores and powder for my ship" Mr. Denholm said, "You have been a friend to the company. It is time to return the favor. Mr. Chambers would you look into Captain Burnes's needs. I'm sure we can help the Navy out. You came to our aid when we needed it. We shall give you the best we have and happy to send the bill to Admiral Grayson." Robert felt relieved and turned the discussion to his days in command of *HMS Seahawk.* They had a delightful dinner together. The John Company would make arrangements to deliver his full request of stores to the *Peacock* in the morning. Robert's biggest problem at the moment had been solved.

The next morning the Admiral called all Captains to report to the Port Admirals office at eight bells in the morning watch. The entire staff was there to deal with all the shortages. One by one the Captains stood up and stated their problems and complaints against the port's support facilities. Admiral Grayson tried to resolve as many issues as he could. Then he realized that Captain Burnes had not spoken at all. "Captain Burnes of the *Peacock* I know you have not had time to even get to your ship yet. What issues do you have with getting your ship supplies?

Have the port facilities been cooperative?" Robert stood up and reported. "I have no issues with Victualing, Stores, or the Armory Sir. I will assume that the water hoy will be available today or tomorrow. I understand that the ship's company is undermanned, however, I am sure that every Captain in this room has that problem." All the Captains in the room looked at him with amazement. The Admiral asked one more time. "You have no supply problems and the ship will be ready for sea on a moment's notice." Robert answered with a simple "Aye Sir." Admiral Grayson thought "I wonder how he pulled that one-off. He is a very resourceful officer." Grayson then dismissed the group but asked that Captain Burnes report to his office at two bells in the afternoon watch. Everyone in the room bet he was going to get an ass chewing. None of them were prepared to get to sea.

Robert on his return to the inn saw Mr. Hicks standing outside with four sailors. Mr. Hicks reported, "Look who I found." Robert with surprise said, "Smith how good to see you." His mates looked at him with a who is Smith look. Smith, happy to see the Captain said, "We heard that the fleet might be in need of a few sailors." Robert answered, "Aye that is true and in fact, I am looking for a new Coxswain. Would you be interested?"

"Aye Sir, I would be honored," He looked at his mates "Me and the Captain sailed together on the *Seahawk*. We got a lot of prize money sailing with the Captain. That were a fine ship were it not Sir?" Robert nodded and said, "Indeed it was Mr. Smith. I will give you the appointment and to any of you, I will also give a berth in the *Peacock*. Be here at the turn of the watch this afternoon and we shall go aboard. Mr. Hicks my pantry will need stores for a six-month cruise." He gave him £60. Get us the very best you can. We will meet here at the turn of the watch.

Robert was off to see the Port Admiral. The port office was still in turmoil. Lieutenant Grayson was there to greet him. "Good morning Sir," Robert had a big grin on his face. "Ah, Mr. Grayson you look well." They entered the Admirals office. "Sir Robert. Right on time. I have your orders for you, but first I must point out that you are out of uniform again." Robert was puzzled. "I believe you became a Post Captain with three years seniority yesterday. Why are you only wearing one epaulet on your right shoulder? Mr. Grayson take the Captain's jacket and see to it. Now on to your assignment. You will take word of the opening of hostilities to your old hunting grounds: Antigua, Barbados, and Jamaica. Here are your dispatches for each. You are to get there in all hast. However, the outbreak of war will be a surprise to the French so any opportunity you find to capture French-flagged ships would be most appropriate. Here are separate orders allowing you to do so and to send them here to Plymouth. The press is not in authority yet so I can not help you there." Robert stated, "I have run into some old shipmate and will have twenty or so prime hands to take on board today. However, if you have some spare Marines and Sr. Midshipmen, it would be most helpful with prizes we capture along the way. Admiral Grayson asked, "Would you mind taking on another Lieutenant?" Robert sensing the request said, "I would be honored to take Lieutenant Grayson with me." Before leaving the Admiral had to know. "How did you get the necessary stores for your ship on such short notice?" Robert replied, "The John Company is our friend Sir." They both laughed. "Good hunting Sir Robert. I will keep Blackwell here as long as I can."

"Aye Sir. Thank you." Lieutenant Grayson appeared with the jacket with the proper rank.

Robert asked, "Are you ready to get to sea."

"Aye Sir. My sea chest is in the hall." The Graysons, uncle, and nephew said their goodbyes. The secretary advised that ten Marines would be at the wharf in one hour along with three Midshipmen. Robert thought to himself, "I love it when a plan comes together. I HAVE A SHIP!"

HMS PEACOCK

Six Bells in the Morning Watch

First Lieutenant James Bradford was up at first light. The ship had been anchored here for the last six weeks while his captain went up to London to attend Parliament. He worked the crew every day. The ship shined with new paint and you could see your face in every piece of brass. The crew was getting restless, but the boatswain had a handle on it. This was not a happy ship, but he had not conducted a flogging since the Captain left the ship. The Captain's nephew Lieutenant Alsop was back. He was known as the snitch by the crew. Promises had been made by Captain Blackwell, with his contacts in Parliament, that would ensure he got his step after this commission was over. He had served with Captain Blackwell for three long years now.

There was a knock at the gun-room door. "Sir, the officer of the watch has requested that you come on deck. There is a John Company barge alongside with forty barrels of victuals for the ship." Lieutenant Bradford called for the purser. The purser said, "Per the Captain's instructions I have ordered nothing for the ship. There must be some mistake. This is John Company stores." The bargeman handed him the paperwork. It was for the *Peacock* all right. Bradford called for the boatswain to get the victuals on board and stored away. Mr. Alsop wanted to put his two cents worth in but Bradford would have none of it. Every ship in the harbor was getting ready for sea as the *Peacock* just sat there. Something was up. "Purser, make sure it is all put on the books."

At noon the powder hoy came alongside. Bradford asked, "Who ordered powder?" The master of the barge had no idea. The gunner was called. He looked at the paperwork and said "Sir I did not order anything. The magazine is almost full as the guns have not been fired in many months, but this is very good fine powder. I will find room for it." Lieutenant Bradford had no idea what was going on.

Within the hour the store's barge appeared. It was also from the John Company. The manifest had listed six months worth of rum, sailcloth, and sundry items for a long cruise. Bradford consulted with his Second Lieutenant Alsop who had no idea what was going on. Then the water hoy showed up with orders to fill all casks. Bradford commented to Sailing Master McGregor. "Something must be up. We have full stores to set to sea."

Lieutenant Bradford had no idea what was going on. He called for his Captain of Marines. "Captain Stark with his sergeant saluted. "What is our complement of Marines at the moment." He thought, "Good God the man is pickled midday." Sergeant Higgins reported, "Six in hospital. We are short nine privates at the moment."

"Thank you, Sergeant Higgins." Stark just smiled. Bradford thought, "I am thirty-six short of full complement at the moment. The ship has just been supplied for a long journey by the John Company which is unheard of. Something is going on and I don't think Captain Blackwell knows anything about it." He looked to the officer of the deck. "Advise me immediately if the admiral sends any signal to any ship." He went below.

At the end of the afternoon watch, the First Lieutenant was summoned to the deck. "There are three boats pulling for us Sir. As the boats approached the boatswain called, "Ahoy there" The answer came back, "*Peacock*." Bradford ordered. "The Captain is back. Form the Marines.

Boatswain, prepare to pipe the Captain aboard." The First Lieutenant prepared to greet his Captain with Lieutenant Alsop at his side.

Post Captain Sir Robert Burnes climbed to the deck, saluted the quarter-deck, and marched down the line of Marines. Lieutenant Bradford Saluted. "Good afternoon Sir. I am Lieutenant James Bradford welcome." Sir Robert introduced himself and presented Lieutenant Grayson. He looked to the Marines and recognized Sergeant Higgins. He nodded at him. Captain Stark thought the nod was for him and nodded back. Captain Burnes took charge. "Mr. Hicks, Mr. Smith please get my stores aboard. Mr. Bradford have the purser sign in the new hands. I have also brought three additional midshipmen and ten Marines. After you have taken care of this please join me in the great cabin."

"Aye Sir. Please follow me to the cabin." Robert with Lieutenant Grayson followed him. As he went into the cabin he could not believe his eyes. The cabin looked like the bedroom of a bordello. There was a tapestry on the wall. The floor had a very expensive carpet. There was a full bed on the Larboard side. It had parlor furniture, a dining room table and chairs, a full desk, and a large wine cabinet. Robert was stunned. His only question was, "WHERE ARE THE GUNS?"

The First Lieutenant returned. Mr. Hicks and Mr. Smith were bringing Roberts' sea chest and personal effects into the cabin. Lieutenant Bradford reported, "Sir all the new hands have been signed in. We are now only fourteen short of a full complement. The Marines billets are now full with one additional.

There are now six midshipmen aboard. All provisions are stored. Welcome aboard again."

Robert looked at his surroundings and laughed. "I wish to meet all officers commissioned and warrants here. Then assemble the ship's company and I will read myself in."

"Aye Sir" within minutes the group was assembled. Robert looked to the group. "I am Sir Robert Burnes, your new Captain. Regrettably, Captain Blackwell has been delayed. I suspect we will be at war with France again tomorrow or the next. This ship is not ready to face the French. The morning meal will be at first light tomorrow. Have all hammocks piped to the netting by then. We will then hold divisions and inspect the whole ship. Advise the galley they are exempt from this inspection. Now Mr. Bradford where are the guns that should be in my cabin?"

"They are in the hole, Sir. Captain Blackwell had them removed when he permanently bullheaded the cabin." Robert should not have been surprised. "I wish to have the bulkhead returned to naval standards and the cannon returned to their proper place. All this furniture will be stored in the orlop. The boatswain spoke up. "The Captain ain't gonna like that and the desk and wine cabinet will not fit." Robert looked to the man and could see the hate in his eyes. "You forgot Sir on the end of that statement boatswain." He then heard a sarcastic "SIR".

Robert could see that Smith's fists were clenched and was about to bounce. Robert said, "Stand to Mr. Smith!" Robert looked to his First Lieutenant but saw no reaction. "Very well. Assemble the ship's company. I will read myself in." He thought to himself "He had a lot to do and needed the support of everyone in this cabin."

A FIGHTING MACHINE

Start of the second Dog Watch

Robert returned to the cabin and invited his First Lieutenant. Mr. Hicks poured two glasses of port and left the cabin. "Let's be frank with each other James. You and I are about the same age yet you are a senior Lieutenant and I am a Post Captain and it is true that we must serve our masters. I have had the pleasure of serving with some fighting officers. Men who look for action and have a good eye for the gun. Blackwell has served his time like he is the captain of a sailing yacht not a man of war. I am sure he has made promises to you. He is a politician first. They only lie when their lips are moving. This is a fighting ship and I intend to make it so. The crew is not with us James. They have been beaten into submission. We must gain their trust and demand the best from them. I will not serve in a sullen ship. Are you with me First Lieutenant

Bradford or not? We have a lot of work to do and no time to do it. I can make no promise to you other than my success will be your success. We will make this into the instrument of war the King intended. The decision is yours, Sir! You must decide now!"

They looked each other square in the eye. The moment of truth had come.

James answered, "You are right. The last three years we have pretended to be in the King's Navy and this flogging disgusts me. Blackwell could make me or break me and I am the lesser for it. I am with you, Sir. The Blackwells of the world be damned."

Robert had his answer. His First Lieutenant was with him. "At first light let's get busy. The war will not wait for us and I intend to be the first ship out of this port. Thank you, James!" Now he must write to Catherine. It might be his only chance.

> *My Dearest Catherine,*
>
> *It has only been a few days, but I miss you terribly. I think of you at sunset and the health of our unborn child. It gives me joy to think there will be three of us soon. By the time you get this letter war will have been declared and I will be off to alert the stations in the West Indies, an area I know well. I have a frigate of 24 guns, the HMS Peacock. It appears it will be a six months*

cruise or longer. I pray I will be home for the birth of our child. The ship is not in the best of shape, but we will work hard to bring it to fighting trim. The crew is another issue. The Captain who gave me the lash many years back, Blackwell has also been the most recent Captain of this vessel. The crew has been beaten into submission. I believe I have the support of the First Lieutenant who is very capable. I also have young Lieutenant Grayson with me. He sends his regards.

The sailing master Mr. McGregor is a very professional sailor. We shall get to know each other better. My Captain of Marines is a drunker. I am afraid he will not be of much help. However, the gods have blessed me with Sergeant Higgins who served with me when we took the Kazidor. He is a fine fellow and a good Marine. The surgeon is a lifelong professional so there should be no problem there. The purser is another question. I have never found one that was not a crook. The boatswain is my biggest problem. He is one of the followers of the previous Captain and a very sadistic man who is very hard on the crew. He controls them with an iron fist. I must get the crew on my side. A good boatswain is worth his weight in gold. A bad one can sink your ship.

Fear not. I will deal with the problem.

I am afraid that this will be my only letter to you my love until I see you again. Say hello to the whole family. My regards to Molly and Tom. I pray the time goes fast.

I love you with all my heart. Be well until we meet again,

Sincerely,
Robert

The good Captain was up before first light and to his amazement so was Mr. Hicks, who brought his pan of hot water to shave and have a cloth bath. He had his back to the door when the Marine guard announced the First Lieutenant. James walked in to give his morning report, but was stopped dead in his tracks by the lash marks on his Captain's back. "Forgive me, Sir!" He was embarrassed. Sir Robert turned to him. "Ah yes so you see. It happened on the *Hermione* when I was a midshipman. It was another lesson for me that there are always lesser human beings than ourselves." James looked to his Captain. "Blackwell had the *Hermione* back in 94." Robert smiled. "He did indeed. We can't go backward. Look only forward. Let's get this ship in fighting trim. James did not know what to say other than to nod. "Aye Sir."

Robert got dressed and went on deck with his First Lieutenant to face the day. At first light the hammocks came up to be placed in the netting. The crew then went to breakfast. Mr. Hicks came on deck with a pot of coffee. The two people who were about to shape the future of the *Peacock* drank their coffee and watched the sunrise.

When the sun was fully up Robert said to James, "Let's begin." The First Lieutenant called to the boatswain, "Pipe the ships company to divisions." As the whistle sounded the crew scrambled to their positions. The boatswain and his mates were using their starters like they were herding cattle. The Captain could not stomach it and said, "Belay that! Stop thrashing the crew immediately. Damn your eyes!" The boatswain looked to the quarter-deck with hate in his eyes. Mr Smith came to the Captains side. The First Lieutenant reported. "The crew is formed. All are present."

Robert walked past the Marines in scarlet. He then moved to the main deck and walked down the line looking every man straight in the eye. He then moved to the gun deck inspecting every gun. "Number one gun is unserviceable. Number two gun the touch hole is painted over. Number three gun. Where is the rammer?" He went down the line reporting every error and then called for the master gunner and the armorer. "Call the gun crews down here. Have each stand by their gun. "Every gun will be serviceable by the end of the watch and I will reinspect at the end of the Forenoon watch. Boatswain get the guns out of the hole. Call for the carpenter to get to work on the cabin bulkhead." Lieutenant Bradford dismissed the ship's company from divisions and advised, "There will be no grog until the ship is ready."

Captain Burnes returned to the quarterdeck. The whole crew was in motion. "Good morning Mr. McGregor. Would you join me in a cup of coffee?"

"Aye Sir. I would indeed." As the whole ship went to work on the guns and moving Blackwell's household goods to the orlop the good Captain asked Mr. McGregor, "Why is it that every Sailing Master I have served with is a Scotsman?" McGregor said with humor, "Well Sir, the Admiralty has not seen fit to make us Admirals so it has fallen to us to keep his Majesty's ships headed in the right direction." Robert laughed. "Well said. I have had the honor to serve with a fine Scotsman." McGregor spoke, "Aye Sir. We are a small community in the Scottish Highlands and we all know of you and William McDougall's exploits in the Sugar Islands. I knew him well. The current charts have his passage on Guadeloupe well marked and we thank you, Sir." Robert wanted to change the subject. "How long have you served with Captain Back-Lash?" This brought a smile to McGregor's face as he said, "You know him well, Sir!" The good Captain responded, "Up close and personal Mr. McGregor. Up close and personal."

The crew of the *Peacock* worked very hard to get the ship ready for war. The cabin was brought up to naval standards. By mid-afternoon watch, all guns were serviceable. Robert noticed that the boatswain and Lieutenant Alsop were having a number of private conversations.

Robert called all the officers to the great cabin and included Mr. McGregor. He wanted the new chain of command understood by all. He laid out his plan. "The fourth Lieutenant and a midshipman would command the Larboard guns. Mr. Alsop and a midshipman would command the Starboard guns. Lieutenant Grayson will command the gun deck." Mr. Alsop interrupted. "Excuse me Sir. I am Second Lieutenant on this ship." Robert asked, "What is the date of your commission, sir?" Alsop answered, "17 May 1800." Robert looked at Mr. Grayson. "And you Lieutenant Grayson?" Grayson answered, "7 January 1799." Robert said, "Well, that is settled. Mr. Alsop, you are a third of this ship. Any questions. I expect three accurate broadsides in five minutes. That is our standard. We will exercise the guns every day until we meet that standard. Thank you. Dismissed." Lieutenant Bradford remained. "Sir the gun deck is ready for your inspection." The ship was now looking like a man of war.

UP ANCHOR

Six Bells in the Forenoon Watch

The harbor had become very quiet. There was very little boat traffic. The whole anchorage was standing bye. All the ships were watching the haliard at the harbor office. Sir Robert was watching the signal tower on top the the hill outside the port. He was using the see'em long glass. There had been no semaphore traffic all morning which was unusual. Robert asked McGregor, "How long until the tide changes?"

"We are an hour and a half until the start of the ebb Sir." Robert ordered, "Mr. Bradford we shall go to a single anchor if you please."

"Aye Sir. All hands up starboard anchor." In ten minutes the boatswain reported, "Anchor is up and down." Bradford ordered, "Break it haul and cat." He waited and then reported to the Captain. "Sir, the starboard anchor is catted."

"Very well." Robert still had his glass on the Signal tower, but could not see incoming signals, only outgoing being sent on to Falmouth. A horseman started riding hard toward the port.

Robert ordered, "Mr. Bradford up anchor." He responded "Aye Sir. All hands up larboard anchor."

The Captain ordered, "Mr. McGregor prepare to get underway."

"Aye Sir, I will bring us round toward the quay and clear the rest of the ships at anchor. Then take us directly out to sea." The Captain answered, "Very well" as he continued to watch the signal tower for an outgoing message. The Mids were watching the signal hailard at the Post Admirals office. The Captain said, "There is the signal. Flags hoist our number and acknowledge." Bradford reported, "Larboard anchor is up and down." The Captain responded, "Very well. Break it and cat."

"Aye Sir." The Captain looked to Mr. McGregor. "Take us out." McGregor looked to his Captain with a wink. "Aye Sir. Lads man the braces. Man the jib halyards. Set the jib and hoist away." Then he looked to the helmsman. "Helm amidship." He replied, "Helms amidship Aye." The sailing master was in his element. He grabbed the speaking trumpet. "Make ready to set sail." The Captain just watched the harbor entrance and the jetty. He was estimating angle, tide drift and wind. He smiled at McGregor as the ship came alive. McGregor ordered, "Let fall the foresail." The top men were like a ballet in motion. "Lead along topsail sheets. Let fall I say." To the other mast he ordered "Clear away fall. He then looked to the idlers and Marines. "Hall the sheets lads."

Mr McGregor reported to the Captain they had steerage way. The Captain ordered,"Very well. Four points to starboard." McGregor looked to the helmsman. "Four points to starboard Aye." McGregor had the speaking trumpet in hand. "Let fall the mainsail. I say sheet it home. Sheet it home."

The signal gun fired at the Post Admirals office. The signal was raised. The flags Mid reported, "Signal reads War Declared. Get to Sea." Mr. Bradford was concerned that they were headed for the head of the larboard jetty. Robert smiled at the sailing master. McgGregor thought to himself, "Our skipper is a real sailor and likes to cut it close." The wind, tide and canvas pushed the ship to starboard. Mr. Bradford was relieved. McGregor said, "Headed full and bye Sir." The *Peacock* was free of the land. This man of war was headed in harm's way.

Robert said, "Well done Mr. McGregor. Stay on this heading for three leagues. "The First Lieutenant asked, "Should I set the watch Captain?" Robert looked back toward the harbor. No one was following. They all would wait for the change of the tide. "Stand by Mr. Bradford. As soon as we clear the land we shall beat to quarters and exercise the guns. Dinner will be late tonight." Robert went to his cabin. He was back at sea!

Admiral Grayson called his secretary and staff into his office. "How many ships have put to sea?" The harbor captain reported that only the *Peacock* had left at the signal gun. The rest were waiting on the tide and would be at sea within the hour. The signals Midshipman rushed in and said, "The signal station reports gunfire about three leagues from the port." The staff looked quite concerned. Admiral Grayson just smiled. "That will be Captain Burnes exercising his guns. He hopes to be the first frigate into the channel where the hunting is best." He needed a hundred more like Burnes!

THE HUNT IS ON

Six Bells in the Morning Watch

It was daylight. The *Peacock* was off Penzance. The lookouts were up and they had just finished the morning exercise with the guns. The Captain told McGregor "Take us deep into the French side of the channel." They were alone. Not another sail to be seen. The ship cruised all day. The Captain, First Lieutenant and the Sailing Master were deciding their next move when they heard from the lookout, "Deck there. Two sails off the Larboard quarter." Everyone in the ship was instantly on alert. Robert glassed them. "Mr. McGregor we will close on the sails.

French colors if you please. Mr. Bradford we will beat to quarters." The ship was alive with activity. As they drew close the lookout reported, "Deck there. They are French. Both have three masts. I believe they are Merchantmen." As the *Peacock* approached, neither made a move to run or evade. The Captain smiled. "This is too easy. Show them our colors. Run out the guns. A speaking trumpet if you please." Both ships heaved to. Robert in French gave them the sad news. In less than an hour the prize crews were on board with three Marines in each. They had a Midshipman in command and written orders from the Captain to head to Plymouth with all haste. As soon as they were in friendly waters they were to hoist English over French colors to be sure no English man of war mistook them. As luck would have it they did have contact with two ships that had been at anchor in Plymouth with the *Peacock.*

As the *Peacock* turned South Southwest Mr. Bradford who had led the boarding party reported. "Both ships were fully laden. One with cow hides for leather. The other was full of French wine. I relieved them of a few cases to ensure quality before it gets to England." The Captain responded, "Well done. The crew will be in prize money. Extra grog ration all around." The only man on the ship who seemed unhappy was the boatswain.

They were six days out when the lookout reported, "Deck there. Ship fine on the bow. Looks to be a liner fully loaded." As she spotted English colors the French ship tried to run. The *Peacock* caught up to her in half an hour and two shots across the bow were all it took. Sir Robert spoke to them in French that they were now the property of the King of England. War had been declared. Two boats were put over the side. Sergeant Higgins and Lieutenant Bradford took over the ship. It was full of cargo from the orient. Half the crew were from the East Indies and swore allegiance to the King with a promise of release when they reached England.

Robert had a problem with this capture. He did not want it to fall back into French hands. He ordered Mr. Alsop to the cabin with his last remaining Sr. Midshipman rated master's mate. "Lieutenant Alsop here are your orders to take command of that vessel. You are to proceed directly to Plymouth per my orders." Alsop asked, "Why me Sir?"

"Having command of a captured ship will look good on your record. By the time you reach Plymouth your uncle will be there. It is evident to me that you want off this ship. I shall accommodate you Mr. Alsop. We will heave to here until you are over the horizon to insure your safety. Get underway as soon as possible. Safe journey."

"Aye Sir" was his only response. He packed his sea chest and left the ship. One of Robert's problems had been solved. He knew the Boatswain was losing control over the crew and now had lost his only ally. All they talked about below deck was the prize money. Mr. Smith was keeping him appraised.

They cruised on for three more days then the lookout reported, "Sail on the horizon at about fifteen leagues." The Captain knew this would be a long chase and that their primary mission was to get to the West

Indies as soon as possible. By now the French would have ships at sea to get the word to their garrisons in the Caribbean. Robert ordered, "Mr. McGregor we will maintain our course and put some more sail up. Waste not a minute." The crew was disappointed.

They pushed on for a week. Then the Boatswain made his move. At the start of the first dog watch there was a commotion on deck. The Boatswain with his two mates had Mr. Smith between them and his head was bleeding badly. Lieutenant Bradford had the deck. The crew was coming up to see what all the commotion was about. The Captain was called from his cabin. The Boatswain made his report. "Sir, I am charging this here man with assault on a noncommissioned officer. It is a capital crime and I demand justice. My two mates will swear to it. I knows the regulations Sir." Robert knew he would have to handle this correctly or there would be a court of inquiry when Blackwell took over the ship. He called for the Sergeant at Arms to take Mr. Smith to the surgeon. He told the Boatswain to put it in writing. "I will call for defaulters at eight bells in the morning watch." The Boatswain knew he had the upper hand.

Then one of the seamen spoke up. He was skinny and had no teeth. "Begging your pardon Captain, but ain't none of that is true. I saw those two strike him while he wasn't looking. Those two and the Boatswain have been stealing from the crew since I've been aboard and that's the truth." The Captain said, "Bring that man forward." Robert could see that the whole ship was watching intently. "Your name." The man replied, "Georgie Philpot Sir. I'm with the Larboard watch"

"You saw the Mates strike Mr. Smith, my Coxswain." The man was very nervous but replied, "I did your Lordship and that's the truth. They have been stealing from the crew for as long as I've been on this here ship and there is a special punishment for thems that resist." Lieutenant Bradford asked, "Is there anyone who will support this man's story?" The Boatswain jumped in. "It's a lie. This here man has had ships punishment twice. He's a no good." Now Robert had to act. "Sergeant at Arms take this man in your custody. Make sure nothing happens to him. We will resolve this at eight bells in the morning watch." The Boatswain smiled. He had it under control. This was his ship! When Captain Blackwell gets back there will be hell to pay.

Mr. Smith was taken to the great cabin. The surgeon said, "He has a hell of a bruise on the back of his head. Smith said, "I'm sorry Sir. They blind sided me as I came out of the head. Robert told him, "Bunk next to Mr. Hicks tonight. We will resolve this in the morning."

It was the Second Dog watch. Sergeant Higgins came into the great cabin without the usual announcement from the Marine on duty. Captain Burnes looked at him. "Is there a problem?"

"Aye Sir. I just saw the Sergeant at Arms take that seaman Philpot to the orlop. I think they intend to change his mind about ratting on their extortion scheme." The good Captain was surprised. "The Sergeant at Arms is in on it!"

Sergeant Higgins said, "I am afraid so Sir. I have two of my most trusted Marines outside. I think we should hurry!"

They quietly moved below the gun deck to the bilge and orlop. It was very quiet. The three Marines had their bayonets locked on to their muskets. Captain Burnes led the way. Up forward was a light and the muffled cries of a human being. The Boatswain's mates had him held down. The other man was holding the light, while the Boatswain was using his persuasion stick on poor Philpot. From the darkness the Captain said, "Dear God. What goes on here?" The Boatswain by reflex reached for the knife in his belt. That was a mistake. Sergeant Higgins lunged his bayonet into him and fired a round for good measure. The Sergeant at Arms before he could assist got his head bashed in by the second Marine.

The gun shot got the whole crew up. Sergeant Higgins called, "All Marines to the gun deck." Then Robert called, "Surgeon to the orlop." He was helping poor Philpot to his feet. The Marines dragged the Boatswain's mates from the orlop and put them in Irons. Robert called to Mr. Bradford. "Take charge here. I want a complete search of their areas. Find their stash." Robert went back to his cabin followed by Sergeant Higgins. Smith and Hicks were waiting there. "It is dealt with and I am sorry it has come to this. They got what they deserved." Robert looked at all the officers entering the cabin. "Where is Captain Stark?" Mr. Grayson answered, "I am afraid he slept through it all. He tied on a big one today Sir." The crew now knew the two biggest thugs in the ship were dead. They felt for the first time like free men. Well as much as you could be free in the Royal Navy.

PLYMOUTH HARBOR

Start of the Afternoon Watch

Admiral Grayson had only one ship left to get to sea. It was coming out of the yard today. He had to send three ships to sea with Jobbing Captains on Admiralty orders.

The port's effort to get ships to sea was paying off. There were three captured French merchantmen sitting in the harbor and one eighth of the prize money would be his. Two of the prizes were taken by the *Peacock*. His secretary advised him that a heavily laden French vessel was now coming into the harbor. He also stated that Captain Blackwell was most insistent on having a meeting. The Admiral said, "Tell him after lunch and send a signal that the temporary Captain of the prize should report to the Port Admiral's office.

Captain Blackwell left to go to the inn. All his followers were waiting outside. He thought to himself,

"That large French ship will be worth a lot to the captain who captured it." The harbor boat was pulling from the ship with the prize crew on board. He did not recognize anyone but kept hearing, "Uncle, Uncle." To his amazement it was his nephew Lieutenant Alsop. Blackwell thought, "What the hell is he doing here." As he climbed from the boat he said, "Uncle I brought that ship in! The *Peacock* has captured three French ships. There will be prize money." Blackwell asked, "For Who!" He was angry. Alsop said, "I must report to the Port Admiral." Blackwell followed him in. Admiral Grayson didn't bother with the Captain. He looked to the Lieutenant. "Well Lieutenant, you have a report for me?"

"Aye Sir. I am Lieutenant Alsop of the *Peacock*. I was ordered to bring the prize to Plymouth by Captain Burnes." The Admiral asked, "Did they try and run?"

"Oh indeed Sir, but Captain Burnes had the weather gage and fired two shots across the bow. That is all it took. Half the crew was East Indian and the Captain had them swear allegiance to the King. The ship came in without trouble." He gave Captain Burnes orders and report to the Admiral. Blackwell had enough. "Sir, when will my ship return to port?"

Grayson was going to have some fun with this arrogant man. "Well Captain Blackwell the *Peacock* has done well with three captures. I am afraid that your ship will not be returning to port. It is under Admiralty orders to take the alert to the West Indies."

Blackwell was now upset. "Who gave those orders Sir?" The Admiral said, "The First Lord of the Admiralty did. Perhaps the First Lord will have another ship for you Captain." Blackwell knew there was no point in lingering here. There must be a convoy out of Spithead going to Barbados or Jamaica. He must get to Portsmouth. He left without saying a word. Admiral Grayson looked to the young Lieutenant. "Get along with your uncle."

The Admiral returned to his desk. "I guess that went pretty well." as he chuckled to himself. "I think I will send a note to Sir Robert's prize agent at Lloyd's. He has done well indeed."

CEREMONY AT SEA

Two Bells in the Forenoon Watch

The *Peacock* was deep into the Bay of Biscay. It was a somber Sunday morning. It is a custom to hold Divisions, inspect the ship and hold religious services or read the Articles of War to the crew. The two bodies were sewed into sail cloth sacks with two cannonballs at the feet of each. There was a sail laid out on the deck with over two hundred items owned by the crew. The purser and the clerk John Hicks were at a table to record who claimed each item. There was a Boatswain's dress jacket and hat, a symbol of the rank of the leader of the lower deck, placed on the quarterdeck in front of ships company who were at divisions. The rest of the day was called a make and mend day. Not today.

Mr. Bradford called the ships company to attention and advised that all were present or accounted for. Captain Burnes announced, "Very well, Ships company Off Hats." Robert moved to the main deck by the bodies. They were laid on planks with members of the crew by each side ready to slide them into the deep.

Robert was short and sweet. "I hereby commend your bodies to the deep. May God have mercy on your souls!" The bodies were lifted. Robert said, "Wait! Where is the cat of nine tails?" (The Lash) which had been so feared on this ship. Seaman Philpot Larboard watch answered, "I will get it." and ran below deck, retrieved it and brought it to the Captain. It was even in a red bag.

Captain ordered the men to proceed. They slid the bodies over the side. Robert threw the bag which had caused so much pain and suffering over the side with the bodies. "Hats on." He proceeded back to the quarterdeck and looked to the crew. "This ship needs a new Boatswain." Robert then ordered, "Andrew Clawson step forward." Robert had asked Mr McGregor who he felt would be a good leader for the men. McGregor's only candidate was a profes-sional sailor, captain of the main tops, and had been a boatswain in a brig before coming to the *Peacock*. Mr. Bradford had the same recommendation. He then asked Mr. Smith who told him it would be a good choice as the men respected him. Robert spoke to the crew. "Lads, I present you with your new Boatswain. The crew gave him three Huzza's. Robert gave him his coat and hat of rank and asked him to join the other officers on the quarterdeck.

Robert turned his attention to the items on the canvas. "I wish items that were taken from you to be returned. The roster will be called and each of you will identify and recover your property.

You will then state to Mr. Hicks how it was taken and sign or make your X." Many came forward to claim that money was taken. Mr Hicks would return it using the Captains funds if it was not on the canvas. Things moved along and the crew was dismissed from Divisions to enjoy the rest of the day. The tension in the ship vanished. The gunnery continued to improve. Everyone jumped to their task. Sail drill was done with precision. The *Peacock* was sailing full and bye toward the eighteenth latitude and the turn toward the West Indies.

CATHERINE IS NOT WELL

Four Bells in the Afternoon Watch

Catherine had decided that child baring was not for sissies. She had to admit that her sisters were right for once. Being with child at a younger age had its advantages. Both twin sisters seemed to have breezed through without any issues. They had gone to London four months along. They came home, had their little girls, and were back to normal life.

Catherine had started getting sick in the morning soon after Robert left. She was tired all the time. Her back was killing her and now she feared something was wrong. There was not much movement in the child. Abigail, Mimmie and aunt Betty were hovering around her all the time. They were worried.

Catherine and her mother decided to visit the closest doctor located in Exeter. He was a university trained physician. He examined her and was quite frank with his comments. "Your slim curvy frame may be attractive to your husband but is not very suitable for child birth. I can see you are having a rough time." He took a glass cone open at both ends and placed it on her belly and listened with his ear on the other end. He looked to Catherine. "The heartbeat is strong. I suspect that you are much further along than you think. The child is small but appears to be well formed. I would recommend that you get as much rest as possible and curtail all household activity." Catherine told him that she was the school teacher in the village. The doctor said, "I would recommend that you limit your time." He looked to Abigail. "How experienced is the midwife in your village?" Abigail was surprised by the question. "She has been taking care of the village for some years." The doctor said, "Madam I believe the birth will be difficult. I hope she is up to the challenge. Now my dear I shall bleed you, which will help rejuvenate your vitals. They had planned to go shopping after the visit to the doctor. Catherine was very tired and wanted to go home. She slept on her mother's shoulder all the way to Riverton. Abigail was very concerned.

CLOSE HAULED

Six Bells in the Morning Watch

The ship was settling in. The tension was gone. They were close hauled on a Larboard tact. The crew was experienced and Mr McGregor was very attentive to sail trim which carried over to the officer of the watch. The glass was holding steady. Captain Burnes was still on his guard.

Expect the unexpected. The sailing master commented, "I believe we will have a few days of fine sailing Sir." It was a fine morning and the Captain was making it his routine to ask the officer of the watch and midshipman to breakfast with him. "Aye Mr McGregor. Would you join us for Breakfast?" He answered, "Delighted to Sir."

Mr. Hicks had everything ready. The midshipmen on this ship were well fed. They received the same rations as the crew. They were usually very quiet at breakfast. Lieutenant Grayson was officer of the watch. He and Mr McGregor were always trading barbs. There was a knock at the door and the Marine announced the First Lieutenant. Robert said, "Good morning James. All is well?"

"Aye sir. Log reads nine knots." Robert sensed that the Lieutenant had an issue. He dismissed the midshipman. "What's on your mind?"

"The two we have in irons must be dealt with Sir."

"Agreed. What do you have in mind?" James didn't say anything. Robert looked to Mr McGregor and said, "Flogging will not solve this problem. The crew needs to have the final say on those two. Call for defaulters at the end of the watch."

At the end of the watch most of the crew not on watch stood as a group on deck. Robert had Sergeant Higgins bring the two on deck. They both could see that the grading was not set in place. It would not be a flogging. Robert looked to the two. "Do either of you have anything to say." Silence was all he heard. "Very well. I am reducing both of you to ordinary seamen.

Boatswain assign one to the larboard and one to the starboard watch." Then the bigger of the two spoke. "You are signing out death warrants Captain." Robert was speaking to the crew more than the accused. "If you make amends to the crew they will accept you. If you do not then the balance of your time on this ship will be hell. It is up to you. Boatswain take charge of these men." Robert looked to his First Lieutenant and said, "It will be lower deck justice James. They made their bed. Now they must lie in it. Officer of the deck dismiss the company."

They had two days of good weather and few issues. Gunnery continued to improve. On the third day one of the punished men fell from the main mast, hit his head on a spare and fell into the sea. The ship heave to, but nobody was spotted. On day five during a squall at night the call "Man overboard" was heard but again no man was spotted. The letter D was marked by their names on the ship's roster. No more questions were asked.

They reached the eighteenth parallel and found the trades. They were headed due west toward Barbados. The Captain and First Lieutenant kept the crew busy with small arms drill. The Marines became the instructors. Lieutenant Grayson showed his swordsmanship by leading cutlass drill. The crew could now fire the guns three times in five minutes. *HMS Peacock* was now in fighting trim and the crew took pride in their man of war status.

The gun room held a dinner in the Captain's honor. They were eating ships fair. They all sat down and discovered that they had no wine. Captain Stark, half in the bag already said, "No problem. I have a key to Blackwell's wine cabinet." Off he went and returned with five bottles of fine french wine. It was a happy dinner. Mr. Bradford commented, "These John company victuals are the best he has seen in all his years in the

Navy. Every barrel we open is fresh and top of the line. A well fed crew is a happy crew." Robert had seen an amazing transformation of the ship and crew since he read himself in back in Plymouth. His First Lieutenant was on top of everything. Mr. Grayson was correcting all deficiencies on the gun deck. The third Lieutenant was learning his role. The surgeon was on top of his profession. He had a most excellent Sailing Master. His only shortfall was his Captain of Marines. If he was not in the bottle by noon it was a good day. However Sergeant Higgins made up for that shortfall in spades. He was starting to think it would be hard to let go of the *Peacock* when his jobbing Captain days were over. They were lifting their glass. "To the King here, here."

It was a full two weeks before they had Barbados in sight. They headed around the point into Carlisle Bay. Robert ordered the signal WAR DECLARED as they entered the bay.

On the Flag ship the Flag Captain asked the midshipman of the watch to ask the Admiral to come on deck. "What number is that frigate?" They checked the signals book. The flags Mid sail, "*HMS Peacock* Captain Blackwell Sir." The Admiral Sir John Clifton arrived on deck. The Flag Captain said, "Sir, It would appear we are back at war and that Captain Blackwell is the messenger." Sir John answered, "Oh really. I would think he would be in Parliament making as much noise as he can. Maybe he is more of a sailor than we thought. Signal Captain to repair on board the Flag."

On the *Peacock* Mr. Bradford and the Boatswain were getting the cutter in the water. Smith was instructing the crew. Marines were at present arms. Robert went over the side with the dispatch bags.

On the Flag they piped the Captain aboard. The Flag Captain was surprised it was not Blackwell. Captain Burnes introduced himself and was escorted to the great cabin. Captain Burnes entered the cabin and he was surprised to be greeted by Admiral Clifton. He said, "Sir John it is good to see you again!"

"Well Captain Burnes congratulations on your knighthood. Well deserved. I won't ask where Blackwell is. Let's get at those dispatches." His servant gave the good Captain a glass of port. As the Admiral read the dispatches he handed them to his Flag Captain to read. After he was done, he looked to Robert, "Do you have any additional information?" Robert replied, "It was all done so very quickly. I was appointed Jobbing Captain. We caught the French completely by surprise. I put to sea as quickly as I could. We captured three French merchantmen in just a few days. We could have captured more, but headed here as fast as possible. I am ordered to get to Jamaica with all speed. The only other thing I heard was that the Admiralty is putting together a convoy to reinforce the islands. I am not sure how soon it will be here."

The Admiral ordered the Flag Captain to get his last Brig ready to sail to Antigua with the dispatches for them. "I would offer you dinner, but I am sure you want to sail with the tide to get to Jamaica."

"Yes Sir John, but I have one other issue to discuss with you. He handed over the report of the Boatswain's death and the extortion ring he had uncovered. There was also the testimony of the crew and all the valuables found. Sir John read the report. "If I know Blackwell I believe he will find a way to resume command of the *Peacock*. He is close to making Admiral. Maybe he will not be able to get here and I can give you permanent command. We can only hope." Robert responded, "Aye Sir John I know him well. I served under him and still have the scars of that commission."

"I shall keep this report in reserve so to speak. Now after you have carried word to Jamaica, I would like you to check on your old hunting grounds around Martinique and Guadalupe and see what are French friends are up to. I will expect to see you in six weeks and hopefully give you permanent command of the frigate." Robert was very happy. "Thank you, Sir John."

"Good hunting Sir Robert. I will have your orders in a few minutes." Captain Burnes was on his way. Within the hour they were weighing anchor and on their way to Jamaica. The ship and crew were in good spirits. Sailing full and bye Indeed.

OLD HUNTING GROUNDS

Six Bells in the Morning Watch

M r. McGregor had made a perfect landfall. They were off the Western tip of Guadalupe island. "Well done Sailing Master. Mr. Bradford we shall beat to quarters. Hoist French colors if you please. I would like all midshipmen with their journals." In a few minutes the First Lieutenant reported, "Ship is at quarters Sir. All midshipmen are present."

The Captain looked to his students. "Gentlemen, We are entering the Straits of the Saints. A great battle was fought here commanded by Lord Howe. We shall travel up the South side of the island, which is in enemy hands. That is Fort Vieux on the Western tip. You will note that the fort is signaling to the next Fort on Grand Arse to starboard. It is important to note even in peacetime these forts are keeping good look out and signal discipline. They will soon know we are at war. To your starboard are a small group of islands. There is a passage through those islands only on Royal Navy charts called McDougall passage." He winked at Mr. McGregor. "It may save your life someday." They moved further up the channel toward the island of Marie-Gatante. The Captain checked three land references and said, "We will heave to here Mr. McGregor."

"Aye Sir."

Mr. Bradford said, "Why are we stopping here Sir?" The Captain responded "In tribute to a ship."

"I see no ship Sir." Robert looked out the stern for a long moment and said, "That is because it is forty phantoms below us!" The gun deck was nervous and was looking out the open ports. Mr. Grayson who knew the story from his Uncle stood by the ladder on the gun deck so he could be heard by all. "Fear not lads. Below us is a British Sloop of War of 16 guns. Some four years ago it took on a French National frigate of 32 guns and won the day. Unfortunately the *HMS Seahawk* was lost in the action. That ship was commanded by our Captain."

The Captain then said, "Sailing Master let us get underway. We shall look into Port of Point a Pitre on Guadeloupe and get out of these confined waters." They looked into the port. The lookouts reported no man of war present. "Gentlemen the French use these waters to their advantage. Be alert if you travel these waters again." The Captain told the mids to return to their duties. "Mr. McGregor let's put some more canvas up and head into open waters. Secure from quarters Mr. Bradford. Let's look into Martinique and see what we find there."

The next day they were off the West side of Martinique. They were flying French colors. The *Peacock* sailed past Diamond Rock and the fort. The fort dipped her colors to the ship. Robert ordered, "Mr Bradford we will respond. Let's get as close to the harbor as possible." They were less than a league from the harbor.

"Deck there. Count six ships in harbor. One is a seventy four. All are bare polls. No sails visible." The Captain had all the information needed." Ware ship. Mr. McGregor let's get past the fort. I wish us to head for the windward side of the island and head for Barbados. We are nine days overdue. There is nothing to see here."

TROUBLE AT THE COTTAGE

Two Bells in the Afternoon Watch

Catherine was in labor and it was agonizing. Aunt Mimmie asked Rosie to fetch Mrs. Hancock and Betty and have them come to the cottage quickly. Aunt Betty got the midwife. They were all in consultation on what to do next. The midwife, their local expert, thought that the ladies were over doing it. There was no rhythm to the contractions. It was too soon by her judgement.

Catherine was in intense pain.

They waited all afternoon timing the episodes. The midwife was right, but they did not stop and were a lot longer in duration. Then the midwife inspected the tummy and with concern told the ladies that the baby is in the wrong position. "It could be a breach birth", which the midwife had never done.

By this time Lambert, Lord Eastman, Uncle George and Davies were in the parlor wanting to do something. Catherine's screams of pain were all on their minds. They asked what could be done? Abigail's only comment was, "I wish the Doctor was here." BOOM! All the men beat to quarters. Lord Eastman said, "I will get my coach. There is not a moment to lose." Davies announced that he was going with his Lordship. Lambert asked, "What if he can't come?" Davies gave him that man of war look and said, "Oh he's coming alright. Make no mistake about that." Davies went to get his best blue coat and his navy service pistol. Lambert offered to help Lord Eastman. In less than a minute the men were gone. The house was quiet until Catherine had another episode. Abigail knew this was not normal and she remembered the Doctors warning. "Her frame is not meant for birthing babies."

Uncle George went to the inn to ask Molly to take over the inn. Molly and Tom were outside the smithy. Molly, hands on her hips, was asking, "What's the gun for?" Davies told her, "Never you mind. We are going to get the Doctor." Molly shook her head and said, "MEN" and went to the Tally Ho.

In fifteen minutes Lord Eastmans coach and four were at the smithy. Tom jumped aboard and they were off. Lambert went to the cottage and asked Abigail, "Is there anything else they could do?" Abigail was afraid to ask. She just smiled and went back to Catherine. The midwife did not know what to do. The birth canal was not opening. The water had not come. The baby was in the wrong position and the contractions were irregular. In her opinion this was not going to end well and she was going to get the blame.

On the road to Exeter the coach was flying. The two passengers were bounced around at an alarming rate. Lord Eastman was instructing the driver, "Faster, Faster I say." They arrived in Exeter just after dark. Lord Eastman instructed his coachman to go to the stable and switch to fresh horses. He didn't care about the cost. "Be back in ten minutes. Let's go get the Doctor Davies." They knocked on the door several times. Finally the Doctor answered. Lord Eastman in his most persuasive manor explained the urgency of the situation and money was no object.

The Doctor was quite put out and told him matter of factly he could not make the trip at night. Tom Davies, gun captain of number six cannon on the *Thunder* took over. There were no negotiations. He drew his pistol. Pushed it in the Doctors stomach and said, "You'll be coming with us Sir and that ain't no error." The Doctor reached for his bag and heard, "What is the commotion dear?" The Doctor said, "There is an emergency. Please don't wait up." The coach and four pulled up out front. Davies told the good Doctor to get in. They were off. Lord Eastman told Davies, "You can put that pistol away before you shoot the Doctor." Davies said, "Sorry your Lordship, but don't worry. It ain't loaded." His Lordship laughed. The Doctor was not amused.

The coachman pushed the horses. They got about nine miles from Riverton and the coach slowed. The coachman reported, "One of the horses has come up lame or has thrown a shoe." Davies jumped from the coach to check the horse. Lord Eastman said, "Don't fool with it. Just cut the animal out." Davies got his seaman's knife out and cut the harness off. "Just leave it. We will deal with the horse later." Davies joined the coachman to be sure they had no more problems.

They were off again. Time was running out. Waste not a minute. Aye Sir. They were three hours from home.

DECK THERE

Two Bells in the Afternoon Watch

"Deck There, Three sail fine on the bow at about ten Leagues." Mr Bradford called for the Captain and said, "Lookout what course?" The lookout responded, "Opposite course. Looks like a frigate and two merchantmen." Bradford reported the situation to the Captain. Robert glassed them and told the deck, "We will close on them." In a few minutes the lookout said, "Deck there. She is an English frigate. The two merchantmen are turning to the Northwest." Mr. Bradford said, "I'll bet he spotted our French colors and wants to do battle. Boy will he be disappointed." Robert went to the bow to get a better look with his glass. Mr. Bradford joined him. "James, what would he be doing here on a course for Martinique? Robert hollered back to the quarter deck "Mr. McGregor put some more canvas up. We will close on them. James we shall beat to quarters."

The deck was cleared. Mr. Bradford reported, "Guns are ready in less than eight minutes Sir." Robert responded, "Very Well. Lookout what do you see?"

He responded, "Deck There, she is definitely a British Frigate. About our size." There could only be one answer. Sir Robert said, "We'll now. The only English frigate that is in French hands that I can think of is the *Lightning*. Mr. Bradford strike the French colors and put ours up. Within a minute, "Deck There! She is turning away from us to the Northwest."

"Mr. McGregor plot an intercept course if you please."

"Aye Sir. We are about fifty minutes from Sunset."

"Mr. Bradford you have the deck. Put our best lookouts up. We will be in darkness before them. I wish to know if they turn and what direction. Mr. McGregor let's get the charts out and plot our best estimate of where they are."

The *Peacock* sailed on for 30 minutes. Then the Captain ordered, "Let's turn the ship toward Barbados." At sunset the lookout reported, "Deck there. The frigate is turning back West." Robert smiled at McGregor. "Now we will see how good we English navigators are!" McGregor smiled. "Indeed Sir"

LIFE HANGS IN THE BALANCE

Two bells in the evening watch

Although they are 2,700 nautical miles apart, Lady Catherine and Captain Robert Burnes will be tested and on this night of nights. Both lives will hang in the balance.

"Godspeed Catherine."

"Godspeed Robert."

HMS PEACOCK Robert checked the chart one more time then stated, "We will heave to here Mr. McGregor. I believe we are at the intercept point. Mr. Bradford put your best lookouts up and a Mid with the night glass on the main mast."

"Aye sir"

"I want all the lights out and complete silence. Captain Stark have all your Marines remain below deck. Officer of the watch hoist French colors if you please." He looked to John Hicks and smiled. "Everyone remove your uniform jackets and hats. We are now a French ship." All was quiet except the gentle swell rocking the ship. Time seemed to stand still. Then the silence was shattered. "Deck there. I can see lights fine on the larboard quarter."

BLACK STONE COTTAGE After examining Catherine the doctor advised Abigail, "The baby is not in the breech position. I believe it is sideways in the womb. At this point I see no movement in the child. We must perform a cut in her belly to remove the child. It is called Cesarean and has been used since ancient times. I have done this procedure twice. I have saved the mother once. Both babies were still born. Should I proceed madam?"

Abigail looked to Mimmie. She was very distressed. "Yes doctor, please save my daughter!" Abigail went down stairs to inform Lambert and the others of the grave situation.

The doctor said to Mimmie, Aunt Betty and the midwife, "I need all your linens, towels, and clean white cloth. Our biggest fear is that the young lady goes into shock. She has been in distress for too long." Catherine began to scream with the latest contraction.

Abigail returned and the doctor told her, "I am of the new school of thinking. I must prevent bleeding at all costs, but the area must be as clean as possible and I must not inject any foreign materials into her body. Is there any brandy in the house?"

HMS PEACOCK The Sailing Master commented, "That was a fine bit of navigation Sir. The moon will be up in about three hours."

"Thank you Mr. McGregor. Mr. Bradford load all guns, double shot. Do not run out the guns. Prepare all small arms for the boarding parties. Keep as quiet as possible." John Hicks and his coxswain Smith were at his side with his Marine saber and pocket pistol. Smith also gave him a service pistol for his belt. He called all the officers to the quarter deck. "When this action begins there will be no time to plan. We shall rake him as many times as possible and then board him by the bow and stern. Mr. Bradford and the third Lieutenant will lead the boarding party forward. The Marines, Mr. Grayson, and I will go for the quarter-deck. Mr. McGregor you will remain with the ship and try to keep the prizes from fleeing. Any questions? Let's get to it." He then called Captain Stark to get his sharpshooters aloft. Cutlasses, boarding pikes, axes and pistols were being distributed to the crew. McGregor with glass in hand reported, "I can see all three ships. They are less than a league away."

Captain Burnes ordered a stern lantern to be lit. He then grabbed the speaking trumpet and began speaking in French appealing to the ship to stop and help. The rudder was stuck and English are in the area. They were trying to get to Martinique. It worked. The lead ship, which was the frigate, altered course and were now less than a hundred yards apart. The ship was putting a boat in the water. It was time to spring the trap. "Mr. McGregor bring us parallel to the Frenchman. Show them our colors. Mr. Bradford FIRE AS YOU BARE."

BLACK STONE COTTAGE Abigail was back down stairs. All the family could hear Catherine screaming upstairs. Abigail asked Rosie, "Where is the brandy?"

Rosie replied, "In the sideboard mam." Abigail grabbed a bottle and instructed Rosie to start heating water and to bring all the clean towels and linen upstairs. The men just looked on with concern wondering what the brandy was for? Abigail just smiled and headed back upstairs.

Lambert decided it was not a bad idea. He went to the sideboard, got a fresh bottle, glasses and started pouring.

Upstairs the doctor looked at the four ladies. "I will need all your assistance. It will not be a pretty site. If you are squeamish now would be the time to leave." Abigail stated, "This is my daughter and I will do what is necessary." Aunt Betty looked to Mimmie and said, "We will be fine." The midwife just stood back. The doctor had the ladies strip Catherine naked and place clean linen under her torso. He washed his hands with hot water and soap, poured brandy on his hands, then poured brandy all over Catherine's belly. He took the tools of his trade out of the bag and said, "Let us begin".

HMS PEACOCK They had caught the French flat footed. Three broadsides had been fired into them before they responded. Mr. Bradford back from the gun deck noticed that only six gun ports were now open. Robert looked to McGregor. "They must be en flute. The rest of the guns must have been pulled out of her. She must be full of troops." The sailing master pointed to the French deck. It was filled with soldiers. Robert recognized what was about to happen. "Everyone get down on the deck. Get down now." Two hundred muskets fired a volley at the *Peacock*. The musket balls slammed into the hull or whizzed by overhead. Robert jumped into action. "Mr. McGregor hard to starboard. Mr. Bradford prepare to rake her stern with the Larboard battery." He thought to himself, "This is going to be a tough nut to crack." As the *Peacock* came across her stern twelve guns fired in succession and hammered her stern. Robert grabbed the speaking trumpet and in French told the two transports to heave to and surrender or he would rake them with a broadside. They both dropped their French colors. The two prizes would be in English hands he hopped.

The Frenchman was now turning. Robert looked to the helmsman and told them to stay with them through the turn. Robert ordered "Double shot over ball, both batteries Mr. Bradford. I believe she is going to try and board us." The tables had turned.

BLACK STONE COTTAGE Davies was pacing back and forth in the hallway. Uncle George, Lord Eastman, and Lambert were just listening to Catherine's screams. Then the screaming abruptly stopped. Lord Eastman remembered the night he lost his wife in childbirth, "Oh my God no!"

The ladies looked to the doctor as he stated, "Fear not! She has fainted, which is a God sent at this point." He made the incision on her belly and was preparing to open the birth sack. There was blood everywhere. The ladies were holding Catherine down. The doctor reached in and pulled the lifeless child out and handed it to the midwife. He had no time! His total focus was on getting the birth sack out and to stop the bleeding before he lost the young lady. The midwife wrapped the motionless child in a towel and placed it on the floor in the corner. The doctor was working at closing off the veins and arteries. He felt he was winning. He got his bottle of catgut poured brandy on it and started stitching. He knew he was running out of time. The wound had to be closed quickly.

Down stairs the room was quiet. Lambert wanted to go upstairs, but dared not. You could feel the tension. Then to everyone's amazement they heard the cry of a child.

The ladies looked to the corner and the child wrapped in the towel was moving and letting the world know "I am here!" The doctor ordered the midwife to, "Look to the child." He had a look of disgust on his face. The ladies were overjoyed. Abigail looked to the doctor. He told her "I have done all I can! Start talking loudly to your daughter. Bring her back to consciousness."

HMS PEACOCK Captain Burnes had to rethink his attack. The French had the numbers with all the soldiers on board. McGregor told the Captain, "The Frenchman has made his turn and is beam on to us." Robert had seen this before. *The Kazidor.* He smiled and looked at Sergeant Higgins and Lieutenant Bradford. If the Captain wasn't worried then neither were they.

"James maximum elevation on both batteries. I am not sure which we will fire. Lieutenant Grayson get the rest of the crew organized. We will board the Frenchman. Captain Stark prepare the Marines. I want continuous fire on his quarterdeck." He looked at Mr. McGregor. "Now let's run a bluff. Turn bow on to him. Let's see what he is made of." The Frenchman had massed all their boarders in the bow. The Frenchman tried to turn with the *Peacock* and missed stays. Robert shouted, "We have him. James, fire on his bow as we turn. Mr McGregor wear ship." The sailing master was now in his element. "Aye Sir we will turn about and come up on his Larboard quarter." The *Peacock* fired on the Frenchman's bow gun by gun. It was a devastating blow. They had just evened up the odds. Robert ordered the other battery to fire a full broadside. Then "All hands on deck and prepare to board."

They grappled and Lieutenant Bradford led the crew onto the Frenchman's bow.

Captain Stark, who had been taking a nip from his flask all night, turned to his Marines and said, "You bloody bullocks better follow me by God." He drew his sword and jumped to the French deck. His sword made it. He did not and fell between the two ships. Captain Burnes looked at Sergeant Higgins. "Let's be at em." His only response was "Aye Sir. Marines follow me."

They boarded on the quarter deck. There were French soldiers standing on the ladder. They pointed their muskets at the English Captain. Smith jumped in front and took all four shots and fell to the deck. Higgins and his Marines dispatched all the defenders on the quarter deck and struck their colors. The main deck was mayhem. It was a bar room brawl. Captain Burnes knew they needed to keep the initiative and finish this. He screamed, "FOLLOW ME." It was cut and slash, cut and slash, "PUSH FORWARD LADS." The good Captain was screaming at the top of his lungs, eyes crazed. Hicks was by his side swinging the boarding axe like he was chopping wood. Suddenly he was facing another man. It was Lieutenant Bradford.

"Sir! Sir! It is over. The ship is ours!" Robert looked at all the men, replaced his saber and returned to his persona as captain. "Very well. Well done James! Let's get things organized." He returned to the ship's quarterdeck. There was Smith lying on the deck. Mr. Hicks was by his side. Smith looked at his captain. "We took her Sir. We have been in some sea fights you and me." Robert held his hand. "Indeed we have. Mr. Smith I must know your real name?"

"Arther Kallow Sir." Robert looked to his sailor. "God bless you Arther Kallow." Then he died.

BLACK STONE COTTAGE Catherine could hear her mother yelling at her. She opened her eyes. "Mother why are you yelling at me?" The doctor smiled. Abigail started crying. Aunt Betty brought the child to her. "You have a little boy my dear." The joy in that room could have filled the world at that moment. They all started crying and laughing at the same time.

In the parlor they did not know what to think. Lambert looked to the group. "I think it is good news." Abigail appeared on the stairs. "Gentlemen I have the honor to announce that Catherine and Robert have a son. The doctor is still taking care of Catherine, but things are improving so we are hopeful." The men were shaking hands and then the brandy bottle was passed around. Abigail smiled and went back to Catherine. The doctor had finished his examination and took the three ladies aside. "She is a very strong young woman. The worst is past, but I am still very concerned with bleeding and infection. She must get rest and fluids in her body. She cannot be moved under any circumstances. The dressing must be changed every few hours and use brandy to keep the incision clean. As far as liquids, I would recommend that you find some barley beer or ale and serve it to her very warm. Beer has some healing properties I can't explain." Aunt Betty smiled, "My husband has been claiming that for years." The doctor advised, "You may bring the gentlemen up for a moment only. Then complete darkness and quiet for the rest of the night. I shall find a room at the inn. Call me if there are any issues. We are not out of the woods yet, but I am very pleased with her progress."

Abigail gave stern instructions and brought the men to the bed chamber. Catherine was holding her son. Lambert with a big smile said, "How grateful we are my lovely daughter." Catherine answered, "Father it is my great honor to present to you our son Lambert."

"Oh I am so honored my child." Lord Eastman put his arm on his friend's shoulder. Davies could have busted every button on his shirt. He was so proud. Uncle George just smiled. The next generation of the Burnes clan had arrived. Abigail ordered the men out and to see to the doctors needs at the inn.

The men walked from the cottage to the inn. Lambert exclaimed, "I will pay whatever fee you require. Lord Eastman said, "I will pay double." The doctor said, "I would not have come for the money." He pointed to Davies. "You sir scared the living hell out of me!" Davies shuffled his feet and apologized, but added, "I owe my new life to the Captain and his lady and I will do whatever it takes to protect them." At this point they took the doctor into the inn and Davies returned to the smithy. "We have dodged another bullet Captain and that ain't no error."

HMS PEACOCK The frigate that they had captured was in fact *HMS Lightning.* They sent Marines and a Midshipman to each of the merchantmen. Sergeant Higgins reported that the transports were in fact English and had been taken from the recent convoy. The English crews had been released and now were in charge of their ships. Robert reflected on the day. "It had been a very near thing, but the results were beyond belief." The moon was now rising. Then it hit him." I may be a father by now. I hope all is well with Catherine. We had dodged another bullet as Davies would say that ain't no error."

BLACK STONE COTTAGE The cottage was very quiet. Aunt Betty had left for some much needed sleep. Abigail and Mimmie had cleaned up the soiled sheets and towels. Catherine had fed her baby for the first time and fell fast asleep from exhaustion. The baby was quiet and Mimmie went to her room. Abigail sat in the dining room with a much needed cup of tea. She was looking at the picture of the *Seahawk*. "Fear not Robert we are standing watch here at home. We pray you are safe and well and for your speedy return home."

HMS PEACOCK Lieutenant Bradford approached "Sir what do we do with all the soldiers?" They would be a problem all the way back to Barbados. Robert asked "Are the boats undamaged."

"The one in the water is fine but the one on deck was destroyed." Robert told them, "Get two boats from the transports. Take the oars out of them. Strip all the soldiers of their tunics, pants and shoes. Put them in the boats in their pantaloons. We will tow them behind the *Lightning* and the *Peacock*. Congratulations James I am appointing you temporary Captain of the *Lightning*. Get splicing and any urgent repairs needed. The Larboard watch will sail with you. I wish to get underway by dawn. Have both English Masters report to me." He shook Lieutenant Bradford's hand. "It is an honor to serve with you James. Your courageous conduct will be noticed by Admiral Clifton when we get to Barbados."

"Thank you Sir." His time had come.

THE DOCTOR HAS NEWS

Two bells in the Forenoon watch

The doctor stayed an extra day and pronounced that there was no sign of infection and the baby and mother were doing fine. The ladies devised a schedule with each taking four hours to watch over Catherine. She laughed, explaining that it was exactly like a ship's schedule for changing watch. With Lord Eastman's coach waiting, the doctor made one final visit to the cottage to have a confidential meeting with Lady Catherine. Her mother was present. He checked Catherine and held her hand. "You are a very lucky young mother and have come through this ordeal remarkably well. Your son seems to have all his faculties. It is a blessing. Now other than nursing your baby you must remain in bed and continue to gain strength. The pain will subside in a few days. You have a long life ahead of you. As your physician I must advise you that your first child will be your last. Your ability to become fertile has been diminished by the procedure I performed. I am sorry, but saving your life was my only concern." Catherine looked to the Doctor and said, "I am very grateful to you for all you have done for me and my child. If this is God's will then we will rejoice in what we have. I am blessed by all I have." The doctor smiled. "Good day to you Lady Catherine." Abigail walked him to the coach and he advised he would be back in two weeks to check in on mother and child. As he boarded the coach and four he looked to the stable door and nodded to Davies who gave a naval salute in return. A tragedy had been averted and the family protected. Mission accomplished.

GETTING UNDERWAY

Two Bells in the Morning Watch

The little British flotilla under command of Captain Robert Burnes was headed South-Southwest. *HMS Peacock*, towing two boats with French prisoners, was followed by the newly reinstated *HMS Lightning*, commanded by acting Captain James Bradford, towing one boat full of Frenchmen. The two merchantmen were ordered to follow in good order. To insure they complied with Captain Burnes orders each had a Sr Midshipman and three Marines on board. It was slow going, for *Lightning* was heavily damaged and *Peacock's* carpenter was working night and day on repairs. Robert hoped to be in Barbados in three or four days. His return was overdue. They would heave to at the end of each day to feed the French with ships biscuit and water. They had provided each boat with old sail cloth to keep the underdressed soldiers protected from the sun.

Robert and Mr. Hicks were busy in the great cabin writing the report of their action in great detail. The capture of *HMS Lightning* and return to His Majesty's service would be big news at the Admiralty and would appear in the Naval Gazette. "Mr. Hicks, do we have the number of killed and wounded for the French?" Robert asked.

"No Sir. We just have the count of soldiers in the boats which is 131." Robert asked for the ship's surgeon to report to the great cabin along with the acting First Lieutenant if he is not busy. As they reported Robert asked for the total number of prisoners. Mr. Grayson reported, "*Lightning* has 59 French sailors under heavy guard by the Marines in the orlop." The good Captain looked puzzled. "What was the total number killed?" The surgeon responded, "63 dead Sir." Robert asked, "How many officers were under guard?" The surgeon replied, "None Sir. They are all dead!" Robert looked to Grayson. "Signal the *Lightning* to come alongside. We shall beat to quarters Mr. Grayson. Have Sergeant Higgins get all his remaining Marines on deck."

The ship's company was in motion when Robert came on deck. "Mr. McGregor we shall heave to. Sergeant Higgins every musket must be trained on the French in the boats." Grayson asked, "What's wrong Sir." The Captain looked to his First Lieutenant,

Sailing Master and surgeon and asked, "How many of the French officers from *Lightning* they could account for?"

"The Captain and his First Lieutenant were dead and dumped over the side."

The surgeon responded. "I treated one of the Lieutenants who died this morning." Robert smiled, "Gentlemen where is the other Lieutenant?" As he paced the quarter deck the officer of the watch reported that the gun deck was cleared for action. They all were confused as they looked to their Captain. Robert spoke, "*Lightning* had over 200 soldiers on board. That would mean they would have a Lieutcnant for every twenty to thirty men and a captain for every eighty to one hundred men. The whole unit must have had a colonel in command. That would mean fourteen or so officers. Some of the officers must have survived and are in the boats. All of their officers could not have been killed." Robert grabbed the speaking trumpet and spoke to the *Lightning.* "Mr. Bradford please bring the prison boat alongside. Sergeant Higgins train all your marksmen on the boats." Mr Bradford sensing a problem did likewise. Robert spoke to the boats in French. "There would be no more water or food until all the officers identified themselves and any man found with a weapon would be shot." It was a standoff for quite a few minutes until finally six men stood up. Robert again ordered any weapons to be dumped over the side or they would be shot. To everyone's amazement one short sword, six knives, and eight belaying pins were held up and thrown over the side. Robert ordered the officers to be brought on board. "Clap them in irons and put them in the orlop under heavy guard." An older gentleman asked to see the Captain and as he approached in his pantaloons he bowed to Captain Burnes." Monsieur, I am Colonel Poussard commander and beg my parole." Robert was having none of his treachery. In French he told him "The time to seek parole was at the time of capture and you will be kept in irons with the rest of your officers." Robert looked to the quarterdeck. "We will secure from quarters. Sailing Master McGregor we will proceed on our base course." He smiled. "Ever vigilant gentlemen. This voyage is not over yet." He and Hicks returned to the cabin to finish his report.

The night was uneventful, but the ship and crew were on high alert. They wanted no more surprises. The next morning at the beginning of the morning watch the lookout reported, "Deck there. Ship fine on the bow." The Captain came on deck and Lieutenant Grayson reported. "Sir! She is an English brig of twelve guns and is about six leagues away."

"Very well we will close on the ship. Mr Grayson I believe we have time for breakfast and coffee before he arrives."

"I would be delighted Sir."

As they finished breakfast Robert called for the midshipman of the watch and asked him to signal the brig for the Captain to repair on board the *Peacock*.

Mr. McGregor brought the Lieutenant in command to the great cabin. He saluted. "I am Lieutenant Watson of the brig *Alice*. Admiral Clifton has ordered me to find you Sir. He was concerned that you were overdue. The French have been active and took two merchantmen from the relief convoy." Robert smiled. "Well you have found us. Mr. Hicks a glass of port for our guest. I am sure you will not mind that it is still morning. We have a lot to celebrate. This is my First Lieutenant Mr. Grayson. As you can see the two ships from the convoy are back in English hands and the frigate *HMS Lightning* is back in His Majesty's service." The Lieutenant was shocked. "That is the *Lightning* Sir? I give you joy!" The port was passed around but the Lieutenant was in a hurry to get back to Barbados. Robert looked to the young Lieutenant. "If you would be so kind to take this dispatch to Admiral Clifton and advise him that we should arrive in Carlisle Bay by noon tomorrow."

"It would be my great honor to do so. I almost forgot that there is a very senior captain by the name of Blackwell who came with the convoy. He is most anxious to see the *Peacock* Sir." Robert responded with a smile. "I bet he is. Would you be so kind to fly the signal on entering the Bay that *HMS Lightning* has rejoined the fleet."

"I will indeed Sir!"

The Lieutenant bid them good day and returned to his ship. Robert instructed Mr. Grayson to ask Captain Bradford to repair on board. He needed to discuss Blackwells arrival with him so they both could deal with that very arrogant man. Their last night at sea was very enjoyable as the Captain had an excellent dinner with all his officers. It would be their last night together.

MAN THE BRACES

Eight bells in the forenoon watch

HMS Bodacious, 74 gun Flagship of Rear Admiral Sir John Clifton was at anchor in Carlisle Bay. The convoy from England was landing troops and supplies to reinforce the garrison on Barbados. He had just gotten rid of Captain Blackwell who demanded to know where his frigate was. Sir John knew he had to be handled with kid gloves for he was a member of parliament and on Nibley's finance committee. He was still rereading the dispatch that Alice had brought last night. What outstanding news it was. The black stigma that had been hanging over the Royal Navy was no more. *HMS Lightning* was returning to the fleet.

There was a knock at the door. The Marine guard announced the Flag Lieutenant. "Come."

"Sir the lookout reports four sails approaching around the point." The Admiral responded,

"Have all the ships in the Bay been advised of the tribute?" "Aye Sir. Everything is in readiness."

"Very well. I shall be on deck directly."

Admiral Clifton had served with Captain Burnes and had presided over his acquittal for the loss of the *Seahawk* four years earlier. As he stepped on the deck he thought to himself, "Captain Burnes your good luck continues."

"Admiral on deck" announced the officer of the watch. The Admiral greeted everyone. "It is a good day for the Royal Navy." He could now see *HMS Peacock*, colors flying, followed by *HMS Lightning* with British colors over French (signifying capture) followed by the two merchantmen with British over French colors. The Admiral ordered the Flag Captain. "Begin the salute."

"Aye Sir John. MAN THE BRACES. Signal gun fire." At the sound of the gun all the sailors of the fleet in the anchorage including the merchantmen climbed to their assigned positions on the yard-arms. The *Peacock* began their salute, followed by the *Lightning*. Then the Flag and every ship in the anchorage fired their salute in response. It was a sight to remember.

On the dock Captain Blackwell had just got off the harbor boat when the salute started. His nephew

Lieutenant Alsop advised, "Uncle that is our Peacock being saluted with that other frigate." Blackwell looked in silence. His fists were clenched. "I'll be damned. Someone will pay."

On the *Peacock,* Captain Sir Robert Burnes felt honor for his crew. Everyone was happy with the recognition and the prize money that would follow. He slapped Sailing Master McGregor on the back. "Well done. We shall anchor south of the Flag. Advise *Lightning* to follow Mr. Grayson." As both ships dropped anchor, the Flag signaled *Peacock* and *Lightning's* number and Captain repair on board. The crew with Royal Navy precision had the gig in the water manned and ready. With full honors and Marines at present arms Robert saluted the ship and was piped over the side with three Huzza's from the crew. They rowed to the *Lightning* to pick up Lieutenant Bradford and rowed double quick to the Flag.

Robert was quickly up the side, saluted the quarter deck, piped aboard and marched down the line of Marines at present arms to the greetings of Admiral Clifton. All the officers were clapping. "Sir Robert we meet again."

"Aye Sir John. Allow me to introduce First Lieutenant Bradford who brought *HMS Lightning* in."

"Splendid Lieutenant. Gentlemen shall we retire to the great cabin to observe some refreshments." Robert asked for a few moments with the Flag Captain and Admiral to deal with his prisoners. The Admiral smiled, "I believe that our fleet Marines will be able to relieve you of your cargo. Have the Marine Major deal with it." They spent the next hour toasting in celebration of the victory. Then the Flag Lieutenant cleared the room. Sir John invited Captain Burnes and Lieutenant Bradford to dine with him.

At dinner the Admiral drank a toast to his guests. He then looked to the Lieutenant, "Captain Burnes was very complimentary of your conduct in his report. It is not often that we get to return a ship to the fleet. I will take this opportunity to reward your courage with your promotion to Master and Commander." Sir John passed the parchment document to Commander Bradford. He looked at the document and smiled at Sir Robert. Promises kept.

The Flag Lieutenant interrupted, "Forgive me Sir, but Captain Blackwell is back and demands to see you!"

"Demands you say. Send him in." Blackwell with his nephew in tow entered the dining cabin. "Sir John, I would like to resume command immediately." The Admiral, ever the diplomat, asked Captain Blackwell to join them. He asked Lieutenant Alsop to wait outside. "Have you met Captain Sir Robert Burnes?" Blackwell looked at the scar on Robert's face and responded "I don't believe I have." Robert smiled "We have served together. Do you not remember some eight or nine years back on the old *Hermione* you told then a Sr Midshipman, "You will never make Lieutenant.

You do not have the upbringing or support. I remember as I was leaving the ship I told you we would meet again. Well here we are." Blackwell was stunned. He thought to himself, "This is a big problem. I had this man flogged." Commander Bradford looked to Sir Robert thinking, "Make him sweat." Blackwell ever the politician decided to change the subject. "Sir, I need to assume command of my ship. I also need my First Lieutenant back to get my ship ready for sea." The Admiral now saw his chance to put Blackwell in his place. "Captain Blackwell please see to your ship. Get her ready as soon as possible. The *Peacock* is a welcome addition to my undermanned squadron. You will not be returning to England anytime soon. As far as a First Lieutenant is concerned you will need to find a new one. Commander Bradford will be responsible for the refit of the *Lightning*."

Blackwell was very upset. "Sir, as you well know my services will be needed in Parliament as we go to a war footing again. Need I remind you that I am on the finance committee." Sir John had him where he wanted him. "I agree! If you wish to relinquish your command, I have the most excellent replacement sitting across the table from you." Blackwell almost lost it but held it all in. "I shall see to my ship Sir." He knew if he gave up command now his chances at Admiral would fly out the window, for he was high up the list and was in line for promotion this year or next. Sir John smiled. "Good. See to your ship." Blackwell left in a controlled rage. He would find some way to pay for this outrage. Robert smiled. "Well done Sir John. The Admiral who was always two chest moves ahead spoke his mind. "Sir Robert you are a fine ship's captain, however you have enemies in Parliament and the recapture of the *Lightning* will only rekindle Nibleys dislike and Blackwell will use it to his advantage with the Admiralty. I must get you off this station before he acts." Commander Bradford spoke up. "I have the entire larboard watch from the *Peacock* Sir."

"In your orders I will grant you twenty people, but the rest must be sent back to the *Peacock*."

They finished their meal without further discussion, drank to the King and the defeat of Napoleon. It was a good day.

After dinner Robert asked the guard boat to take a message to the *Peacock* to have Hicks come to the Flagship with his Sea chest and property. Commander Bradford realized that Blackwell had taken the gig so he begged a ride with the guard boat. Robert reflected on the day. It had gone as planned. Always expect the unexpected and he knew Blackwell would not let this go. It was not part of the Navy he liked. Power and control. Oh to be home with his lady at Black Stone Cottage. She was only 2,900 nautical miles away. "I'm coming my love. I'm coming."

THE GOOD DOCTOR

Afternoon Watch

The good doctor was back in town early. Lambert had written him a letter and thanked him for taking care of Catherine and the baby. He offered him a proposal. The village had no doctor so Lambert offered to put him on retainer to visit once per month and take care of the village needs.

He arrived this morning and visited Catherine and was now having lunch with Lambert and Abigail. Lambert had signed an agreement with him and paid him a very handsome retainer for the year. He and Lambert liked each other so another relationship was being formed.

"Your daughter has made a remarkable recovery. If you can you should encourage her to get more rest. She has plenty of help with the child." Lambert smiled and said, "She is an amazing young woman and makes a father proud. Are there any issues?" The doctor pondered this question. "She is healing nicely. There is no infection which was my major worry. I am amazed that everyone in the village asks me how she is doing." Lambert replied, "She and her husband Robert are the lifeblood of our little community." Abigail asked, "Are there any precautions we should take." The doctor decided that she needs to keep her mind active. "I understand that she plays the violin with you Mrs. Hancock. I would encourage that. There is no physical strain and emotionally it will help immensely with her husband at sea."

Later that day the three ladies could be heard playing a sonata from the cottage.

Mr Davies sat outside the smithy listening. Life in the village was returning to normal. Somehow they needed to get a message to Captain Burnes that his son had arrived.

PREPARE TO DEPART

Six bells in the morning watch

The Admiral was up early and requested that Captain Burnes accompany him to inspect the *Lightning*. It was a glorious morning with a light breeze from the Southwest. To Commander Bradford's credit he had a side party ready for the Admiral. He welcomed them and began his tour. Sir John looked at the damage. "This ship has been devastated!" Robert's response was, "Aye Sir. She did not come easy. It was a tough nut to crack with all the soldiers onboard." They were inspecting the damage below the water line with the carpenter when they heard commotion on deck. As they returned to the deck, Commander Bradford was having a rather heated discussion with Lieutenant Alsop of the *Peacock*. Two of their boats were alongside. "What's the meaning of this?" The Lieutenant explained. "I have orders from the Captain to return all the members of the crew to the *Peacock*."

"Commander Bradford did you inform him of your orders?"

"I did Sir." The Admiral now rather perturbed stated, "You are a very impertinent Lieutenant. Follow my orders and return to your ship." Bradford had picked the cream of the crop including the carpenter and his mate plus one of the cooks. The rest of the Larboard watch climbed into the boats but were not eager to return to the *Peacock*.

The Admiral and Captain Burnes returned to the Flagship. As they climbed aboard, standing there was Lieutenant Grayson with two sea chests. Robert made the introductions. "This was my acting First Lieutenant Mr. Grayson." The Admiral bid him, "Welcome! Are you related to Admiral Grayson?"

"Aye Sir. He is my uncle." As they returned to the great cabin the Admiral asked, "So what brings you here? Do you have a message from Captain Blackwell?"

"No Sir. Captain Blackwell asked me to leave the ship and to take Captain Burnes' effects with me." Robert concerned asked, "Where is Mr Hicks?"

"Well Sir. He told me that Hicks is part of the crew and will remain with the ship." Robert protested to the Admiral. "He is my personal clerk and servant and has served with me this last six years. Surely the traditions of the service would apply here." The Admiral was furious. He called for his Flag Lieutenant.

"Mr Ames I need you to go over to the *Peacock* and ask the Captain to release Captain Burnes clerk now." Then Lieutenant Grayson reported, "There is more Sir. Last night Captain Blackwell had a problem with one of the crew. He ordered him flogged. The boatswain you appointed Sir Robert refused to do it so Blackwell had them both flogged." Robert disgusted replied, "That man will never change."

Lieutenant Ames returned. "Sir my trip will not be necessary. Captain Blackwell is on his way to the Flag." Sir John smiled. "I believe Blackwell is coming for his pound of flesh as Shakespeare would say. Mr. Ames have you considered the proposal I put forward last night?" Ames smiled and said, "Aye Sir. I am ready, willing and able." Admiral Clifton was now three chest moves ahead of his opponent. "Is the courier packet ready to sail for London?"

"Aye Sir. It will leave on the tide this evening."

"Very well. Hold it and advise them they will have two passengers for London. Now Mr. Grayson if you would make yourself scarce. Captain Burnes would you retire to my sleeping cabin please. We will see what Captain Blackwell has for us."

The Flag Lieutenant announced Captain Blackwell. Sir John greeted him. "Well you have your ship back. What else can I do for you?"

"Sir my ship is in deplorable condition. There are musket holes all over the upper deck. The great cabin has been completely violated. All my furniture was in the hole. It will take weeks to get it back to my standards. More important there have been violations of the articles of war Sir. My boatswain and Master at Arms have been murdered. Here are my prepared charges against Captain Burnes. He must be held accountable for this crime." The Admiral pulled an envelope out of the draw and smiled. Tapping the envelope on the desk he said, "Are you sure Captain Blackwell. That is a capital crime. Blackwell had another card to play. "My Captain of Marines also died under very suspicious circumstances." He could see that the Admiral was not taking the bait.

"What else do you have for me Captain? I have many things to do!"

"Well Sir I am in urgent need of a First Lieutenant." Sir John smiled. "I have a very capable senior Lieutenant to appoint to the position." Blackwell answered, "I will be happy to interview him." Sir John smiled again. "You do not trust my judgment? There will be no interview. Captain Burnes would you please join us. Captain Blackwell has some very serious charges against you." The surprised look on Blackwell's face was priceless. Robert took a seat. The Admiral handed him the charges against him. "How do you respond to these charges."

"Sir I would agree that the ship when I took command was in pristine condition. The deck shined. The paint work was immaculate. There was not a line out of place. However the cabin was full of parlor furniture, rugs and a full bed Sir. The cabin was permanently bulk headed. I could not get the two cannons required by regulations in there. I removed all of his household possessions to the orlop and returned the gun deck to fighting trim." Blackwell outplayed and tried a desperation shot. "My wine cabinet has been raided Sir. Robert had the upper hand. "Well as you know your Captain of Marines did enjoy his share of spirits. Your pantry should be fully stocked from the stores I purchased. I hope that will compensate for your loss."

Blackwell could see he was not on firm ground. Now Robert wanted to pay him back for the lash he endured many years ago. "However when I assumed command, your guns Sir were in appalling shape. They were painted to high gloss, but had not been fired in nine months. Five were unserviceable and eight had the touch hole painted over. Let me assure you Sir I do love the gun and all were quickly returned to serviceable condition. The gun crews were schooled twice a day until the entire ship could fire three rounds in five minutes. I believe you have the best gunnery in the squadron. As far as damage is concerned the *Peacock* captured three French merchantmen, recaptured two English ships and had the fight of her life against the *Lightning*. The crew gave a good account of themselves. Your ship and crew are a credit to his Majesty's service. Your Captain of Marines was lost as we boarded the *Lightning*. It is all in my report to the Admiral."

The Admiral took charge at this point and still taped the letter on his desk. "I have a full report in my hands with the signed testimony of twenty one of the crew that the boatswain was running an extortion ring including flogging of sailors in the orlop without knowledge of the Captain. This had been going on for months. Months I say! It certainly would not look good on a record of a man about to stand for Admiral. I do have your interest at heart Captain." It was said with a bit of sarcasm.

Blackwell was stunned. He just sat there. His finely tuned plan had failed. He did not know what to say. Sir John was not finished with him yet. "Captain Burnes how many times have you used the lash since you took command."

"None sir. This is a fine well disciplined crew." The Admiral now cautioned Blackwell. "It has come to my attention that people were flogged on your first day back in command. This is unexceptable Sir! I will be watching. You are dismissed. Oh one more thing. The clerk of Captain Burnes will be released to the Flag immediately." Blackwell left tail between his legs. However, he was thinking "I know another way. I must get back to the ship."

Robert said, "Thank you Sir." Sir John looked out the stern windows. "I detest men like him. We must be cautious with his sort. They can hurt us and the Navy.

We must keep them in check. I must get you off this station tonight." He called, "Flags would you and Mr. Grayson step in here." After they entered. "Lieutenant Ames are you ready to assume the position of First on the *Peacock*?" Sir John looked at Robert, "Do you think that Mr. Grayson can step up to my high standards as Flag Lieutenant?" Robert responded, "He is a very conscientious and detailed officer Sir." He looked to Grayson, "Is it the packet back to England or serving me?" Grayson very happily said, "It would be an honor serving with you Sir."

They all left the Admiral to his work and went on deck to the fresh clean air of the bay. Robert asked Lieutenant Ames, "Are you related to retired Admiral Sir Richard Ames?"

"Aye Sir. He is my grandfather."

"I served with him on the *Thunder*."

"Aye Sir. My grandfather Sir James has told me the story of the *Kazidor* many times. I didn't believe all of it until now. With the *Lightning* at anchor it all must be true. They had a long discussion about his days on the *Thunder*.

"Did he tell you about the Marine Sergeant who helped me?"

"Aye Sir. He did."

"Well that man is Sergeant Higgins and is on the *Peacock* at this very moment. He will be a great help to you. It is a small world. Is it not."

"Yes it is. Thank you Sir."

Finally the guard boat approached with one passenger and the mail from all the ships in the anchorage.

Lieutenant Ames grabbed the mail bags and headed for the great cabin. The passenger climbed to the deck. Robert smiled. "Welcome aboard John Hicks. Did you think I would forget you?" Hicks responded, "No Sir, but I was not sure if I would be flogged before you got me off that ship. The Captain and I had quite an argument."

"Well stand by. We will be headed for England tonight."

Robert returned to the great cabin. Mr. Ames was opening the mail bag from the *Peacock*. Sir John asked what was in the bag? Ames replied, "There is a letter to the First Lord of the Admiralty, two letters to Lord Nibley. One is to his home. The other is addressed to Parliament. There is a very thick letter to his wife." Sir John asked, "Any letters from the crew?" Ames answered, "None Sir." Sir John answered, "I'm not surprised. Do you think he writes long love letters to his wife? I think not. I'm sure he is sending the same letters to his wife to be sure they get to Nibley. Well two can play at his game." He smiled, opened the stern window and threw the lead weighted mail bag in the sea. Then he turned to Captain Burnes and shook his hand. "Here are my dispatches to the Admiralty and the mail bags. You will personally deliver my letter to the First Lord and advise him of the capture of the *Lightning*. Godspeed Sir Robert. Have a safe passage home. The courier packet waits for your arrival."

Robert returned to the deck and shook Mr. Grayson's hand. "Good luck. You will do well. Mr. Hicks grab the sea chest. We must be off." The packet sloop was around the point by sunset. The West Indies were at their back. England, London and home were on the bow.

SAFE PASSAGE HOME

First Dog Watch

The two masted sloop rigged craft was a very compact flush deck ship. It was used as a courier packet because it was fast, but lightly armed. It only carried six guns. The Lieutenant who commanded was the only commissioned officer. He had the boatswain move to his cabin and gave the boatswain's cabin to the passengers. They had no midshipmen. One sailor was rated Masters Mate so they could run three watches. Captain Burnes told the young captain he would leave the running of the ship to him, but volunteered to take a watch to help out.

The weather was not cooperating, but did not slow them down. The Lieutenant was not the best navigator in the navy. Robert assisted with the daily position. They all ate ships fare and in shifts of two. Mr. Hicks assisted in the galley.

They came very close to Penzance on the tip of Southern England. He was less than eighty miles from Catherine and his child. The packet continued along the coast, past Portsmouth. On the thirty eighth day they were at the mouth of the Thames. They dropped anchor and waited for a pilot to guide them up the river. The Lieutenant advised they would have to wait their turn for a pilot. Robert felt the urgency of getting to London. Robert asked, "Have you made this trip before?" He answered, "Aye Sir. Many times." Robert now took charge. "Up anchor. Mr. Hicks would you get my personal journal with my notes from our last trip up the Thames." The Lieutenant was nervous but agreed. Robert instructed, "Follow that Merchantman up the river." From his journal Robert gave him bearing and references for his turns all the way up the river. The tide was rising so the passage was faster than normal. As they reached the city Robert asked where he normally anchored. "Wherever I am told Sir." The answer disturbed the good Captain. "Very well we shall tie up to that John Company ship. If they protest you will advise them that you have urgent dispatches for the Admiralty."

A private boat took them to the dock. Mr. Hicks stated, "Well done Sir." Robert looked at him. "I was completely out of my depth on that passage. Divine providence got us here. John do you remember the inn we stayed at last time?

I will meet you there. I am off for the Admiralty."

LIFE RETURNS TO NORMAL

Four Bells in the Afternoon watch

The normal rhythms of life had returned to the cottage. Catherine was feeling much better. Young Lambert was a joy to behold. Abigail and Mimmie were always in attendance. There were no letters from Robert. She was lonely and wanted to share these precious moments with her husband. Life had more meaning. They were now a family. Catherine's life was expanding. She missed Robert terribly.

Lambert and Abigail had stopped by for an afternoon visit with their grandchild. The post rider had just arrived and Tom Davies brought up the mail. "No news from the Captain I am afraid." Catherine said, "Thank you Tom." There was a letter from Robert's Prize agent. Catherine read the letter. "Oh my God!" Lambert, Abigail, and Mimmie looked on with concern. Was it bad news about Robert? Catherine said to her father, "Robert captured three French ships last May and the prize court has awarded £2,900 to him. "I am married to an amazing man." Lambert thought, "He is one hell of a ship's captain." Catherine had returned to health and they had a wonderful grandson.

His relationship with his other sons in law was rather distant. They felt ill used. Young Lord Torrinton lost his income from the business in Winsford. Both daughters no longer received an allowance from their father. Both were jealous that Catherine and Robert were partners in the coal business. It should start showing a profit this year. Elizabeth and Victoria now had a strained relationship with their parents. Their marriages, he had hoped, would unite him with the Lords of the valley, which was having the opposite effect. Thank God for his best friend Sir John Eastman. The good Colonel was always a reality check on life. His military experience was always positive. He was blessed. Abigail was still by his side and always would be. This little cottage that Robert and Catherine called home was comforting and held a special place in their hearts. He knew that in the coming years he would depend more on Robert and Catherine.

Hopefully the love of his daughter's life would be home soon.

OLD JARVIE

Four Bells in the Afternoon Watch

Robert found his way to the Admiralty. As he entered, the hustle and bustle of the place had not changed. He wondered what everyone did? The new First Lord was asking the same question. He approached the secretary who controlled the flow into the inner sanctum. "Yes Sir. What can I do for you?"

"I have urgent dispatches from Admiral Clifton for the First Lord."

"Very well. Leave them with me." Robert put on his best command face and said, "I was instructed to give this letter and the dispatches personally to Lord St Vincent by Admiral Clifton."

"What is in the dispatches?"

"Very good news I assure you. If it is an issue I will wait as long as it takes." He said with a smile. The secretary went into the inner sanctum and returned with a butler. "Mr. Simmons will escort you Captain." He followed the man to the First Lords Secretary. He went through the same conversation with him. He again stated, "I will wait." For an hour he's sat there thinking about the new First Lord of the Admiralty. He was Admiral Sir John Jarvis. The sailors called him old Jarvie. He was a no nonsense spit and polish sailor. "I bet he will shake this place up." Then the secretary came out from the inner office. "The First Lord would like to read the correspondence first, Sir Robert." The good Captain thought, "Well they do know who I am." He handed the letter and dispatchs to the secretary. Another half hour went by. Then a bell rang. Another butler escorted him down the hall to an immense conference room known as the chart room, which had an enormous clock giving time around the world. He approached the end of the table and gave his salute removing his hat and tucked it under his arm. The First Lord continued his work like Captain Burnes was not even there. Then he spoke, "Any Frenchman that sets to sea should fear two Englishmen in a row boat. Good afternoon Sir Robert. You may take a seat."

"Aye My Lord. Thank you." There was no smile on the First Lord's face. In fact there was no expression at all. "You have brought us very good news. I congratulate you on your victory."

"Thank you My Lord." Now old Jarvie had a smile on his face. "You seem to be at the right place at the right time. All good captains are. This scourge. This black mark against the Royal Navy has been erased. Well done. The *Lightning* is returned to the fleet and that despicable young Nibley still walks the earth. Although I believe the Howe family will hunt him down and end his miserable life. We can only hope. If I had my way he would be hanging from the yardarm in front of the whole fleet. Now the question is what we do with you? You certainly deserve a reward. Admiral Cliftons personal letter has outlined the issue for me. The capture of the *Lightning* will be in all the papers and the Naval Gazette. This will open old wounds with Lord Nibley you understand." Robert answered, "Aye My Lord. I do." Jarvie spoke again. "You have earned a frigate and an independent cruise in normal times. These are not normal times. I need to rebuild this Navy as fast as possible and as much as it distresses me, I need Nibley and parliament on my side. Unfortunately for you anything that we could nail a mast and sail to has been put to sea. There are no commands available." Robert said, "If no command is available I would be happy to return to my command of the Sea Fencibles." The First Lord replied, "I am afraid not. It is the beach for you and half pay. Although I understand you did very well in prize money on this cruise."

The First Lord looked Robert straight in the eyes. "You made enemies in Parliament through no fault of your own. I am taking Admiral Cliftons advice and protecting you. Blackwell will still try and hurt you. That man is another black mark on the Navy. We will soon be rid of him, but will still be a member of the financial committee in Parliament. We will make him an Admiral of the yellow, which will mean no seagoing command. Sir Robert you are a fine officer and a good sailor. I understand you have a keen eye for the gun. Go home, and keep low. I will have need of your service again when all this is behind us. This is going to be a long war!" Robert, thinking the interview was over, turned to leave. The First Lord said, "Sir Robert, I thank you! Very well done indeed." As he left he thought to himself "There is more to this than just being a good naval officer. Politics, I hate it. I must stay away from this bloody building. It is not my cup of tea. I must get home to Catherine and my child. Waste not a minute."

A WINTER'S DAY

Two Bells in the Afternoon Watch

It was a cold and rainy Sunday in the valley. Catherine and Mimmie were at the Hancocks residence for practice on a new sonata that the trio were trying to master. Lambert and Lord Eastman were in the study. Young master Lambert was sleeping on his blanket next to the fireplace. The ladies were playing and the men were listening and enjoying their brandy. To Lambert this was the height of relaxation. He was just enjoying his name sake. He exclaimed, "I had no idea how comforting it is to have the next generation of the family before me." John Eastman said, "Dear friend I could not agree with you more." Lambert wanted to be careful with his friend who had no heir to his estate. Lord Eastman looked to the child and his closest friend and said, "Lam that child means so much to both of us for we are both grandfathers and this means as much to me as it does to you." Lambert looked puzzled and was going to ask when the music stopped.

There was a flurry of commotion coming from the foyer. Catherine was screaming with delight and the ladies were crying with joy. Lambert and Lord Eastman left the study to find Lady Catherine hugging the good Captain for all she was worth. "Oh my darling you are safe and home to me." Robert was speechless and just being in the moment. Holding his lady was priceless.

Everyone was watching and Robert was nodding to the family. Catherine grabbed his arm and said, "Come with me and meet our son." They walked into the study. Both quietly got down on their knees before this wonderful child. Catherine had her head on Robert's shoulder. "Here is your son dear husband."

Robert with tears in his eyes said, "He is beautiful my love. Oh God has blessed us." The whole family was standing behind them just soaking in the moment. Robert said, "Please don't wake him. I will just sit here and watch. Thank you my love. This is the most happy moment of our life." Catherine told him, "We have named him Lambert after father." Robert gave his lady a kiss. "How wonderful."

The rest of the family left them to enjoy the moment and went to the parlor. Catherine and Robert were whispering to each other. She began to cry. Mimmie went to watch the child while Robert with

Catherine at his side bid everyone hello. There were hugs and handshakes all around. Robert told them, "As soon as I finished at the Admiralty, Mr. Hicks and I left for home as fast as we could. "Lambert told him, "It is good to have you home. Will you be going back to sea?"

"I regret that the First Lord has thrown me to the beach at half pay for the foreseeable future."

Catherine and I will have to live on love." She was quite happy. The emptiness in her life was now filled. All the agony and worry of the last few months were behind her.

Mimmie came in holding young Lambert. He was awake. Catherine went to change him. She then handed her baby to his father. Robert asked if the ladies could continue playing while he held his son like a fragile piece of porcelain. The three men sat there watching their offspring while the ladies played. What a pleasant homecoming.

John Hicks left the bags and sea chest at the cottage. He went to Tom and Molly's and spent the whole afternoon with his friend telling him of the voyage and capture of *HMS Lightning*.

Catherine fed their offspring and then put him down for his two hour nap. Abigail had dinner ready for everyone. All schedules were centered around young Lambert's needs. At dinner Robert described his almost seven months at sea. Catherine told him of his prize agent's letter which advised that £2,900 was in his account from the captures in May. He told Catherine and the group, "That is only half the story for we also recaptured *HMS Lightning* and the two merchantmen taken from the convoy. I am sure we will be hearing from Lloyd's again." Lambert and Lord Eastman were amazed. Robert's holdings were growing by leaps and bounds.

Catherine's eyes sparkled at her husband. A dark period was over and their life together was whole again. The bed chamber would be warm and comforting. Life had come full circle. They drank a toast to the family and to the health of young Lambert.

THE SURPRISE

The Second Dog Watch

Catherine had her man back. Life was very secure again. There was no worrying if Robert was dead or alive or far worse missing on that gigantic Ocean. He was right here keeping her warm and cozy.

Robert was concerned for his lady. He learned that the birth of his son was a very near thing and it shocked him that her life could have been over. It doubled his affection for her.

Catherine told him "My body has scars now my love." A most serious issue for a lady. Robert laughed. "If you would like to compare scars darling, I have you beat hands down. I will call it your love scare, for it was achieved as a result above and behind the call of duty. We have both escaped serious peril in our lives.

There is a plan for us and I can only see good times on the horizon." Robert was being very careful with his bride. It was the last thing she wanted.

Catherine missed his pleasure with her. Their reunion was a night to remember.

The natural rhythms of the valley returned. The good Captain had his Tuesday luncheon at the Hancocks. Friday morning at first light it was coffee and a smoke with the boys at the smithy. Friday night was reserved to have a wet with the good people of Riverton at the Tally Ho. The quiet of the cottage was never regained. Young master Burnes saw to that. Catherine took to motherhood like a ship takes to sea. It was a happy household. Mimmie was always there to lend a hand. Abigail and Lambert spent many of their Sunday's at the cottage. Their world had changed and all for the better.

Robert's life had exceeded all expectations. When he was a midshipman he could only see as far as becoming a lieutenant. Now he was a Post Captain, Knight of the Realm, and married to the best lady in the land and he loved her more than life itself. He had acquired property and had more money than he could ever imagine. There were also friends that would stand the bonds of time. Now he had a son to carry on after him. There could be no better satisfaction in life. Captain Sir Robert Burnes new life was still full of surprises. Always push forward. Waist not a minute of this precious life.

It was late winter when the surprise came. It was a time of remembrance. He was visualizing the last time he saw his mother alive. It was at the sick house. They were carrying her away outside all those years ago. Now he stood there next to the mound which contained his mother and so many of his neighbors. Catherine was standing by his side with little Lambert bundled against the cold and wind.

Lord Eastman's coach pulled up and he came to the site and stood alone. This lonely man was grieving also for the loss of better times so many years ago. He turned to the couple that he most respected and said, "I regret many things in my life. The loss of your mother is among them. That I sent you away to protect my son Alton is my biggest regret, but you are made of sturdy stuff Sir Robert. The world could not hold you down and when you returned to Riverton as a lieutenant I felt blessed. Now you have made your mark on the world."

Robert looked for a long moment at the man John Eastman. "I regret nothing. The Royal Navy has made me the man I am. My formative years were filled with learning on your estate. I wonder what happened to that remarkable man and great tutor Jean Claude?" Lord Eastman looked to the mound. "He is buried here along with so many others." Sir John Eastman knew it was time. "Robert, you and Catherine are the most wonderful match a marriage could have. We must look to the future. You are my son as you have always been and will always be. Now the three of us must look to the future of my grandson." Catherine could not believe what she was hearing. Robert responded like the words had been used forever. "Of course father. It is time." They boarded Lord Eastman's coach to go up to the estate. They had much to discuss and many a year to make up. Life is always full of surprises. Sailing full and bye on the sea of life.

www.ingramcontent.com/pod-product-compliance
Lightning Source LLC
Chambersburg PA
CBHW051517150726
47997CB00001B/290